Chef's Taste

VIBE *a Steamy Romance*

Series #7

Chef's Taste

Lynn Chantale

4 Horsemen
Publications, Inc.

Dedication

This book is dedicated in loving memory of Percy, guide dog extraordinaire.

You gave my friend Mary Ann 9 and 1/2 years of service. You will be greatly missed and Riley will miss his buddy very much. We love and miss you.

Table of Contents

Prologue

"**O**h my gosh! She's bleeding. She's bleeding!" Jason Michaels yelled. He pressed his hand to the wound. "Hang in there, GG."

This was supposed to be a fun double date, not a scene from the movie *Purge*. Smoke drifted through the space they were in, and he coughed, turning his head into his shoulder.

"The fire is out," Samson "Stx" Denver announced between coughing spasms.

Jason sighed in relief. One issue down; now they had to get out of the building without getting shot.

More coughing drew his attention to his right. "The doors are blocked from the outside," August "Sol" River told them. "And the last window we tried is too small for any of us to fit through."

A boom rattled the air and instinctively Jason ducked, even though he was already on the floor. "What was that?"

"Fireworks?" August ventured.

"Not fireworks," Stx said. He coughed. "Is GG conscious?"

Jason lightly ran a hand over GG's face. Her eyes were closed, but she was breathing. "She's unconscious. And there's a bump on her head."

"I still smell something burning." August couldn't quite keep the fear out of her voice.

"We're okay for now," Stx told her.

"Who has a phone? At least we can call for help."

August crawled closer until she brushed leather, then cotton. Someone's shoe. "Here!" She fumbled her phone into a calloused palm. Briefly, Stx's fingers squeezed hers in reassurance before disappearing. August River continued forward until she found Jason. She nudged him with a towel. "How bad is it?"

Jason shook his head, knowing August couldn't see him. "I don't know. If she would wake up, maybe she could tell us."

"Well, who's shooting at us?" August demanded.

Jason thought he knew but didn't understand why anyone would want to kill him.

"Uh guys," Stx drawled. "We have a big problem."

"Bigger than someone shooting at us and trying to burn us alive?" August quipped.

"Yeah. There's a bomb."

Chapter One

"And go!" a masculine voice shouted.

Jason Michaels pedaled faster on the stationary bike. He gripped the long handles as they alternated up and down. Sweat dripped from the end of his nose, so he turned his head to wipe it on his shoulder. If it wasn't for the built-in fan, which kicked in while he pedaled, he'd be totally overheated.

Some up-tempo rap music blared through the gym's speaker system, a perfect backdrop for the torture, um exercising, they were doing. The scent of sweat, rubber, and other exercise equipment perfumed the air. Around him, he could hear the pants and groans of his fellow companions, which nearly drowned out the spoken lyrics to Eminem's song, "Lose Yourself."

"I'm tapping out!" someone announced off to his left.

"Uh oh! Man down!" Jason called out good-naturedly.

That got a laugh from both trainers and trainees.

"How many more of these rounds?" a woman on his left groused.

"Last one!" Sam, one of the volunteer trainers, promised.

"Thank God!" the woman Jason knew as Sol panted.

Well, he knew her given name as August but had fallen into the habit of calling her Sol. She was one of the few women he dated since his accident. While she had a serious partner in her life now, she provided the comfort and companionship he needed. However, he also desired to have the same serious love she did with her partner.

"I could really go for a plate of nachos right now," August declared.

Jason snickered. Nachos did sound pretty good right about now.

"Rest!" Sam called.

Jason slowed his frantic pace. Every Wednesday and Friday the head trainer, along with a host of volunteers, provided one-on-one exercise support for persons with disabilities. Most of the crew were blind or visually impaired, but a few he knew were in a wheelchair, had leg prosthetics, or other ailments that made a traditional gym more challenging to manage.

He enjoyed these bi-weekly workouts. Not only did it allow him to relieve some of his stress from his day job, but it helped get him in the best shape of his life.

"Go!" Sam hollered. "And make it good. It's the last round."

"Push! Push! Push!" This was from another trainer whose name Jason couldn't remember. Still, for the next forty-five seconds, he dug deep and pedaled for all he was worth.

"Rest!"

Jason let go of the handles and stopped pedaling. He sat there panting as he mopped his face with a hand towel.

"Need a water?" The woman whose name he'd forgotten asked the group.

A chorus of yeses filled the room. Waters were handed out. Jason sipped his while he waited for the next exercise. Scanning the space, he could see movement curved around him. He waited, glimpsing little more than shadows and shapes.

"Ready for those squats?" Sam asked, offering his elbow.

Jason screwed the cap back on his water and felt for the proffered arm. "I'm here; guess I have no choice," he quipped.

"C'mon sandbag," Troy ribbed. "You're not even sweating and you're tapping out?"

Jason grinned. He loved to hear the gruff vet trash talk. "This is just the start of my day, Troy."

"Well sandbag, get to moving. We ain't got all day."

An hour later, Jason was sprawled out on the exercise mat, convinced he'd never move again. He wasn't even sure he could sit up after the five sets of fifteen leg raises and abdominal crunches he just did. He wasn't sure what hurt more: his abs, shoulders, or legs.

"You sleeping on us, sandbag?" Troy teased.

"Yep, just give me a blanket and pillow," he panted.

Laughter flowed around the gym. "Good work, everybody," Sam said.

An hour and twenty-three minutes later, showered and dressed in a pair of black cargo pants and a white chef's coat, Jason shaped a special blend of ground chuck and venison into patties. He set each one on a parchment-lined sheet pan. Once he was done with this batch, he would add the layer of ground bacon for his bacon burgers. Where most bacon burgers had strips of bacon, Jason decided to grind the savory goodness and shape it into a patty as well; that way, each bite held the crunch and smoky goodness of bacon.

A whiff of coconut and lime tickled his nose, which he inhaled appreciatively. "GG, is that you?" he called out, not missing a beat in his work.

"You know it's me," she smirked. "Who else would be stocking this rust box you call a food truck."

"That's no way to talk about your workplace," he chided. "I thought you liked driving our rust box."

"By default," she quipped. "The last time I let you drive, you put a dent in the front fender."

Jason laughed. Indeed, he had put a dent in the fender only because her directions hadn't been clear. "Well, if that dumpster hadn't jumped out at me, there wouldn't have been any damage."

Something heavy shook the worktable. He peeled off his gloves. "Need a hand?" He covered the pan with plastic wrap.

"Uh, yeah," she said, a little breathless.

Jason followed the shuffling and rustling of clothing until he reached the open door of the food truck. Everything from the gourmet burgers, dogs, and brats were ground by hand, then stocked onto the truck. He also had the ability to grind meat on the truck if they ran out of supplies, but that didn't happen very often. Since today they would be visiting a new site, well not necessarily a new site but a new event, he wanted to be sure they could accommodate the crowd, and that meant stocking a few extra raw ingredients.

"Stay there," GG told him. "I'll hand the boxes up to you; it will go faster that way."

"Sounds good."

He did as instructed, hearing an occasional grunt from GG when she handed him a particularly heavy box.

There was nothing sexual in what they were doing, but her little grunt tickled his desire. Blood stirred at the breathy, little sound she made, and he paused with the heavy box in his arms. Would she sound like that if he had her up against a wall, pounding into her softness? Would she still smell like coconut and limes, or something more intimate and primal?

The thought only made his cock harder and long to be deep inside her. He shifted his erection to a more comfortable position as he willed his libido under control. Another whiff of her intoxicating scent though brought his blood to a roar; he stifled a groan. For once he was thankful for wearing an apron, and GG wouldn't know he was sporting a painful stiffy. Deliberately, he set the boxes along the work counter and in front of the table until there was little room to maneuver.

"That's the last one." She shimmied through the narrow opening, brushing against him.

The space was so limited they couldn't help but bump into one another. Jason fought the overwhelming urge to pull her to him and learn every contour of her body. No, he couldn't do that, no matter how much his hormones rode him to do so. He had to maintain their professional air because he didn't mix business with pleasure, and it would definitely be his business to bring GG much pleasure.

"You good?" her sweet voice sliced through his mental fantasies.

"Uh yeah," he answered a little hoarsely.

"You seem a little hot and bothered over there," she teased.

Oh, if only you knew how much. Aloud, he said, "Hoping everything runs smoothly, and we sell out."

She laughed. "Of course, we will." Together, they put away the stock for the day. With the extra food in tow, it was a tight fit but everything was in its place. Jason washed his hands and donned gloves again before going back to shaping hamburger patties. He wished he could work out his desire as easy as he molded meat, but he had to be resigned with a semi hard-on the rest of the day, which was a little surprising for him. He seldom had this type of a reaction to a woman, but his body always reacted to GG like this. Did she know how much she turned him on?

"I'll finish up the dogs and brats," GG said, rattling some dishes.

Now he had the image of her hands all over his particular brat and hot dog. Exhaling, he kept his smile in place and would not think about her stroking the casings as they were almost bursting with ground meat. Instead, he forced his thoughts to her talent. She was good at keeping the business on track, and had a way with their distributors, and the customers loved her.

While he tested and refined the recipes they used in the truck, like the hot dog with finely ground bits of bacon, she made sure he stayed on track. What items they didn't make themselves were the buns; those were made courtesy of PB&J Bakery. Every now and then, the bakery would offer a new dessert or candy to try. Besides, having a gourmet bun for a gourmet hot dog, brat, or hamburger was only fitting.

Soon the scents and sizzling of meat filled the truck. Heat from the fryers warmed his back, while the flat-top grill kept him warm. A crisp breeze from the service window blew through, bringing a hint of rain and burning leaves into the air.

"I've got fifteen orders already, and there's a line of people outside."

Jason grinned. "That's what we like to hear."

A knock preceded the door opening. "Sorry I'm late," a masculine voice announced.

Jason shivered in the sudden chill blowing through the open door. "Not too late, Alistair. GG was just telling me we've got a line going and fifteen orders already."

He heard water run. "That's awesome. I'll get started on the takeout orders and fill in where I can."

"Sounds like a plan."

"I don't get it," Ian Brown said to his companion.

His companion, Dylan Gregor, nibbled on a fruit kabob from a neighboring food truck. All around them, the scents of grilled meat, garlic, peppers, and fried foods perfumed the air. They'd stepped from their food truck, I, Dyne, to scope out their competitors.

All the trucks had unique flair and cuisine, everything from seafood to some sort of Jamaican fusion. His personal favorite was the fried mac and cheese from Mac Attack. The ooey gooey goodness of melted cheese, wrapped in a crisp bread crumb, was to die for.

"We've got a good thing going, Ian. People love our vegan and vegetarian dishes."

Ian huffed. "He gets the prime spot at every event we're at," he griped. "I think they're only doing it because he's blind."

Dylan almost choked on the bite of pineapple. He chewed and quickly swallowed. "I seriously doubt that."

Ian pushed his glasses up on his nose. "Before The Dog Hut came along, we'd be in the spot he's at."

Dylan glanced at their truck, which was third in line from the entrance, to where The Dog Hut was parked across the street and second from the entrance. There seemed to be an equal number of patrons waiting at both trucks. "We're more in line with the herbivore coalition."

"But that used to be our spot!" Ian jabbed a finger at The Dog Hut truck. "Not over here; it's like we've been left to die."

Dylan tried not to roll his eyes but failed.

"See, you're not even taking this seriously. We've lost 1% of our revenue since we've moved to this spot." Dylan finished the rest of the kabob, then tossed the stick into a nearby trash receptacle. "We make that back during football season," he pointed out. "We even have contracts for Dexter Daze, Top of the Park, and Hashbash."

"And I bet we'll be in the back of the parking lot for those events too."

Shaking his head, Dylan walked toward the end of the line at The Dog Hut.

"What are you doing?" Ian demanded.

"I'm going to get a menu and a sample of their food. Maybe it's something we can do a vegan or vegetarian version."

"There's no way to do a vegan hot dog."

Dylan waved him off.

Ian swung back toward his own truck, with his arms crossed and grumbling the entire way. His hand was on the doorknob when a thought occurred. A slow, cold smile creased his lips. He knew exactly how he would get his spot back.

Chapter Two

G G wiped down the stainless-steel prep table with a sanitized towel and stifled a wide yawn, then shook her head to dispel the weariness threatening to knock her out. Today had been busy, busier than she could've imagined. If Jason hadn't had the forethought to bring extra with them, they'd have had to close up shop halfway through the shift. As it was, his forethought kept them going long after some of the other trucks ran out of product. They'd ended out the night with a solitary hot dog bun, and that was because someone ordered a brat minus the carbs.

She cast one last look around the food truck. Every surface gleamed, ready for the next day's adventures. They never kept any real food on the truck in case something horrible happened, like theft or vandalism. Out of habit, she double-checked the fryers were powered down and the oil drained, and properly stored for tomorrow's use. The flat-top grill shone as if it was newly installed. A sense of pride swept through her. Some of her former co-workers thought she was crazy for quitting her job as a chef to pursue a career in food trucks, especially with a blind man.

What her co-workers didn't know was she was secretly in love with Jason, and she'd have followed him anywhere.

With one last look around the interior, GG emptied the sanitizer water bucket, wrang out the towel before stowing the bucket beneath the sink. She carried the towel with her out of the truck. With an elbow, she hit the light switch on her way out and double-checked that the door was locked. She then walked to the driver's side and made sure that was locked as well. GG then circled the truck, checking here and there, before checking the latch was tight and locked for the folding awning and counter. Satisfied, she entered Jason's house.

Jason had converted part of his garage into a commercial kitchen, or, rather, he'd expanded his existing kitchen in two of the bays of a three-car garage.

Even after the long day, she was a little surprised to see him feeding lamb chunks into a buffalo chopper.

GG tossed the used towel into a laundry bag, then stood to watch. At nearly 6'4", Jason always turned heads. But the recent muscles gained from exercising that slimmed down his tall frame kept her in cold showers. He hadn't quite lost his love handles, but they'd definitely smoothed out the last few months. She wasn't overly fond of the chiseled abs and rippling pectorals, preferring her men to have a little meat on their bones, but Jason definitely qualified as having a bit of both. He also had one of those faces that made a woman stare, with deep bedroom eyes and full, kissable lips. She bit back a sigh. On top of the good looks, he had a great sense of humor.

GG studied his face now for the faint tell-tale scars around his eyes. Most people didn't know what they were, but she did. She'd been there when it happened; that was the worst day of her life.

The ballroom sparkled with dazzling crystal chandeliers and expensive diamonds and other precious stones. GG carefully but quickly ladled consommé into warmed waiting bowls. Another cook garnished the pale, golden broth with shaved truffles. She glanced over to find Jason prepping the racks of prime rib to be carved tableside.

This dinner was a big deal, not just for the hotel but for the restaurant as well. It was a big deal because Jason was a partner in the business; his name and reputation were on the line. If the dinner did not go well, she would be out of a job and probably would never see Jason again. GG couldn't allow him to fail or to lose her job, so tonight she brought her A game and made sure everyone else did the same.

Most people thought a sous chef only did menial tasks, like peel potatoes and chop onions. Oh no! She was in charge of the kitchen staff: that meant line cooks, prep cooks, dishwashers, etc. She was responsible for supply orders and would, every now and then, fill in when Jason needed her. It was her responsibility to make sure every dish leaving the kitchen was perfect. And she did it with only the passion of someone who loved an industry notorious for chewing up the strong and spitting out the weak. Not only was being a chef hot and grueling, but it also demanded a lot of physical exertion. Standing for hours on end on an unforgiving floor, no matter how good the floor mats were, added strain to her legs and back. She taken to bi-weekly massages just to keep her muscles limber.

"Roasts are resting," Jason informed her. "By the time we're ready to carve, they will be perfect."

GG wiped a drop of liquid from the last of the soup bowls, double-checked the garnishes, and then waved her hand for the server to take away the full tray.

"Fantastic."

"Since it's such an intimate affair." Jason rolled his eyes as the gathering was anything but. "You and I will carve tableside."

Self-consciously, GG brushed an errant hair from her forehead and had to resist straightening the bandana holding back her kinky coils of curls.

"You have time to change your apron and put on your toque."

Thus attired, when it was time for the main course, they moved to opposite sides of the room. The intimate gathering held fifty of the city's most affluent and influential members of Ann Arbor society, with the guest of honor the mayor of the city. GG could never remember if this was a soft in for a fundraiser or the politician's way of wooing the support of these heavy hitters. What she did remember was a loud crack.

Someone screamed as a sound like shattering glass filled the air. She looked up in time to watch a chandelier fall. Time moved in slow motion. In the time it took her to register the danger, she realized with horror that Jason was standing beneath the light. Did she scream his name? He looked at her, then up.

He was moving, but he wouldn't make it. One tier of the light caught him on the side of the head. The thud and crashing glass on the floor were unbelievably loud.

Jason went down amid the light detritus. His chef's whites were covered in glass, rib roast, and blood.

"GG? You still here?" Jason's voice broke through her reverie.

GG realized she'd been standing doing nothing while the buffalo chopper went silent.

"Uh yeah," she answered. "Truck is ready for tomorrow. Avery called to confirm the bun order, so how about we knock off early and grab a bite to eat?"

Face palm. Did she really just ask him out? She needed the floor to open up and swallow her now.

"A bite to eat?" Jason repeated slowly.

"If you don't want to, it's fine," she rushed out.

"I know it's been a long, busy day, and you had your time with the trainer this morning." And now she was babbling. Why couldn't she just shut up? "I'll understand if you say no," she finished lamely.

Jason turned off the machine and transferred the mixture to a waiting bowl. GG asked him out. *Was it a working thing, or was it more than that?* Hoping she could possibly feel something other than friendship for him was wishful thinking. He carried the bowl to an adjacent prep table where a bevy of spices waited. Once he added them in, he'd place the meat back in the bowl for a final mix before allowing it to rest in the fridge overnight.

He had to admit a small thrill ran through him at the opportunity to spend time outside of work with GG. He remembered what she looked like. She was average height, which put her head at the center of his chest. Her thick mass of curls, always coiffed in intricate braids, knots or twists, dangled well past her shoulders and his fingers always ached to plunder the softness. Coupled with her flawless chocolate skin, she continually had his attention. While she always wore an easy smile, she ran his kitchen better than anyone he'd ever worked with. And she'd abandoned her career to follow him into a food truck business.

Why?

"It's okay if you don't wanna go," she was saying. "It's been a long day."

Indeed, it had, but what was waiting for him at home? A woman he'd been dating was occupied with her new love and son. They didn't have plans to see one another until the weekend. "I'd love to go out with you tonight," he heard himself saying and realized he meant it.

A quick inhale of breath was the only thing he heard.

"But I refuse to let you pay," he told her. "My mama would frown on that."

"We'll see about that," she countered. "Now, what still needs to be done?"

He thought they would never leave. David Foster Marsh glanced at his companion. "Are you sure you want to do this?" he queried.

"I wouldn't have hired you if I didn't. He's dating the woman who should be yours and he's ruining my business."

"And you're certain you don't want me to just blow up his truck?" David hefted the duffle bag a little higher on his shoulder.

"All I want you to do right now is get me into his garage without tripping any alarms."

While David worked on the locks and alarm, Ian kept watch. At the sound of a soft click, Ian turned to find the door opened a mere crack. "Well?"

"It isn't armed," David said.

Ian stalked past him, pulling out a small flashlight. He aimed the beam around the room, surprised at how it looked more like a commercial kitchen instead of a garage.

"I thought we were going to slash his tires or something," David murmured his voice, echoing a bit inside the empty kitchen.

"This will be better. He brags about how his dogs and burgers are all hand- ground. I'm going to give them a secret ingredient guaranteed to kill his business." Ian held out his hand for the bag. Once in hand, he rummaged through it until he came up with a large yellow box with a rodent on the front. Crossing to the large walk-in refrigerator, Ian yanked open the door and surveyed the shelves for what he needed.

Ian was a little surprised or rather impressed at the ruthlessly organized space. Every container was labeled in black marker as well as braille. Even boxes of produce were labeled with dates and times. He bypassed all of these until he found a cart of ground meats; this was what he needed.

Taking off the lid of the first container, he emptied the turquoise green pellets, no larger than a grain of rice, into the mix. He stirred the pellets in to disguise the poison.

He opened another container, this time pouring in a bottle of liquid. He added two more bottles, smiling at the simplicity of his plan. *Get enough people sick, and the health department would shut "The Dog Hut" down until the source of the contamination could be found.*

He then found a large jar of pickles. He added more ipecac syrup to the brine, closed the lid, and gave the jar a good shake.

Glancing around, Ian realized David wasn't with him. He left the fridge the way he'd found it and went in search of his partner-in-crime, finding the other man on his hands and knees examining an indoor smoker.

"Find anything?"

David stood up, wiping his hands on his jeans, mildly surprised at how clean the place was. There wasn't even any grit on his hands. "This place is really clean."

"Yeah, it is," Ian agreed.

"If there was clutter or equipment not maintained, sabotage would be easier."

"You saying you can't do it?"

"I said sabotage would be easier, not impossible," he snapped. "I need to think about this. Get creative with how to destroy the man's business."

"Maybe you can start with his truck. It would be nice not to see The Dog Hut everywhere I go."

They left the same way they entered, making sure all traces of their break-in were eradicated. Ian grinned. He wasn't sure when the meat would be used, but when it was, it would be epic.

The scent of spicy sweet and sizzling meat filled the restaurant. GG watched Jason wield a pair of chopsticks as if he was born with them. They were at one of her favorite places, a Korean barbecue place near Liberty and Thompson in downtown Ann Arbor.

She held her breath as he dipped a dumpling into a mixture of ginger sauce and sesame oil before bringing it to his full lips. The dumpling was the luckiest food right now, touching those full, firm lips. She sat transfixed as he licked a bit of the sauce, then bit into the crescent- shaped food. What she wouldn't give to feel his lips on her. *Would he tease and nibble the same way he did the dumpling, or would it be more aggressive and commanding?*

"This is really good," Jason praised. "I've heard of it, but this is my first time here."

GG brought her attention back to her own plate. "I'm glad you approve. There's just something about being able to prepare your food tableside."

"Even when you cook for a living," he quipped.

She chuckled. "Of course. All I have to do is cook it. Someone else has already prepped it."

Jason laughed, a belly shaking *heh-heh*.

She loved his laugh. It was a bold, boisterous sound that filled the room and made listeners happy and want to be in on whatever joke had caused the outburst.

Tongs in hand, GG placed slices of meat on the in-table grill. The scent of soy and ginger was fantastic. She kept one eye on the grill while studying Jason. The scars, which had lessened with age, were still visible around his eyes, if one looked close enough. Those lines wouldn't be there if the building had maintained the lighting as they'd said instead of using little more than a wire coat hanger and duct tape to hold a heavy light fixture, but now those lines were a part of him, just like his laugh. She wanted to trail her fingers along those lines, then kiss them all the way to his lips.

What she really wanted was to explore his body. He had a tattoo that peeked above the collar of his T-shirt. She thought it may be a bird of some sort, but in all the years she'd known him, she'd never seen it. Quite frankly, the hint of ink on his body was driving her crazy, as she wanted to know how far it went.

"Are you burning our dinner?" he teased.

She looked down to find one of the slivers of pork belly had slipped through the grate, and the fat was burning. She rescued the pork and set it aside. "It's only charred."

He laughed, melting her insides at the sound. Goodness. Where was her mind? Firmly in the gutter if she was fantasizing about touching and kissing. But she wanted more than a few imaginings when it came to Jason.

Jason fiddled with his empty plate, making sure the chopsticks were still balanced across the rim. He slid a hand up toward the left, searching for his glass of sweet tea. His fingers brushed cool condensation, and he wrapped them about the base of the glass.

There was an intimacy in sharing this meal with GG. She'd been the first to reach him after his accident and had stayed with him following the surgery and recovery. It was only after he awakened that he had to force her to go home and rest. *Wasn't that something friends did for one another, or was there more between them?*

He shook his head. The scent of her perfume, mingled with that of their dinner, made his mouth water, not just for food but for the woman. He shifted as blood rushed to a certain part of his anatomy. How would she feel about dating him? Would she be open, knowing he practiced and lived an alternative lifestyle?

"I'm curious," her voice cut through his reverie. "How did you get involved in polyamory?"

He smiled; she was curious and knew exactly what his lifestyle was called. "I started off as a swinger," he explained. "That wasn't quite what I wanted."

"What man can resist such pleasure from willing women?" she teased.

He laughed. "Right. After a while, I wanted more of a connection with the women, not just sex for the sake of sex. Even then, I knew I didn't want monogamy in my life."

"How many partners have you had?"

"The most I've ever had was five. Of course, that was before my accident. Once they learned I was blind, a few of them took that opportunity to sever the relationships."

"Well, that was shallow of them."

He smiled at the censure in her voice; GG cared. "Unfortunately, it's the way people are. Some don't know how to handle catastrophic change."

"Blind or not, you're a good man," she stated stubbornly. "The way you treat women is better than a lot of them get treated."

He tilted his head to the side. "And what do you know about how I treat women?"

Wood creaked and fabric rustled as she shifted in her chair. Was she embarrassed?

"I listened when you would send flowers or other gifts to them. A few times they met you at the restaurant."

Her fingers brushed his, and he grasped them. When she tried to pull away, he held on. Something else occurred to him. "I never talked about my lifestyle at work, so how do you know what it's called?"

A tremor ran from her arm to his fingers. "Like I said, I was curious." Absently, she stroked his knuckles. "I knew you weren't a playa like some of the cooks speculated. You didn't have the drama from the women who came to the restaurant."

"Right."

"So I did some research, spent a few nights conversing with the great Google. It took a bit to figure out the difference between polygyny, polygamy, and polyamory, but there are some great sites out there and plenty of groups on FB willing to share their lifestyle and knowledge to those with an open mind."

Was that a note of wistfulness he detected in her voice?

"From what I gathered," she continued, "polyamory requires more communication than a traditional relationship, but having more than one partner seems like there would be a lot of love and admiration to share. No one would ever have to be alone."

Yes, there was wistfulness and a longing he'd never heard from her before. GG was beautiful. He fully remembered her soulful brown eyes and a mouth worth kissing. Many of her male counterparts made quiet noises about wanting to date her, but Jason didn't allow fraternization in his kitchen. He'd seen too many shifts deteriorate when a relationship went south.

"I always thought you were pretty lucky to have so much love."

Jason didn't know how to respond to her statement. He'd never thought of himself as lucky in love, but he was fulfilled in loving the ones he did. Did she not have the same experience? Even in a traditional relationship? He twined her fingers with his. "You're an intelligent, beautiful woman, GG. Any man would be a fool to let you get away."

Clothing rustled as she shifted. He could almost see her blush and duck her head.

"I wasn't looking for just any man."

Her admission set his heart racing. She couldn't mean him. For a moment, he pondered her actions over the last couple of years. There was one huge thing he had to know.

"Why did you quit the restaurant to come work for me?" he asked suddenly. He wasn't sure why the question was so important now, but it was. He had to know the reason she followed him. "Had you stayed, you'd been promoted to my old position, and someone else would've been your sous chef."

"We're a team," she answered.

He caressed her knuckles with his thumb. Her skin was petal soft, and he enjoyed touching her. "That's not exactly an answer," he said huskily.

She squirmed in her chair, though she did not try to pull away again. In fact, she held his fingers. "Let's just say I couldn't imagine being in the kitchen without you."

She couldn't imagine being in the kitchen without him. He let the statement play on repeat. She'd been there when she didn't have to, and now they were holding hands at a Korean BBQ joint.

"You don't feel the same." A note of hurt clung to her tone.

"What if we explore what's between us and it fizzles?" he countered. "I wouldn't want to ruin a perfectly good partnership. Besides, I cannot offer you a traditional relationship; it isn't in my makeup."

"We'll take things one day at a time. There's no reason we can't maintain a professional air in the truck," she assured him.

His heart leapt at the words. For the first time in a long time, well since losing his vision, he believed he could have a solid relationship with another woman. He hadn't lied to GG; at one time, he did have five partners. After his accident, there was only one, and she didn't care that he was blind. All she cared about was the way he treated her.

"I like your lifestyle, Jason. It's different, and I believe I'm strong enough or at least open enough to pursue what we have."

He smiled; *this could work after all.*

Chapter Three

G G stood on the house stoop, the box of leftovers in a bag over her wrist. Jason stood in front of her, fumbling with his key. She knew from experience not to ask him if he needed help. Actually, now that she thought about it, she didn't hear the jingle of keys, but a series of beeps.

"You got a new lock?"

He chuckled. "August, that's the other woman I date. She talked me into getting a keyless entry. What she didn't tell me was when the batteries go and I don't change them right away, I have to use my key."

"August?" GG savored the name. "What's she like?"

"Sassy, independent, and has a big heart. She'll like you." He stepped aside so she could enter. "She has a live-in love, but I'm not sure if he's proposed to her yet."

GG closed and locked the door and traversed the short hall into the kitchen. "Will I get to meet her?" She placed the leftovers in the fridge. "I put the box on the second shelf, lefthand side."

She turned to find Jason in her personal space. He was so close she could smell his aftershave, a blend of citrus and pine. The heat of his body bled into hers. She closed her eyes, savoring the nearness. They'd worked in close quarters before, but this was different. They weren't boss and subordinate, but man and woman. The thought was freeing and scary all at the same time.

She pressed her hands to his chest, marveling at the firmness there. A sigh left his lips, and it warmed her right down to her toes.

"I hope you don't think this is too forward, but I've been wanting to do this for a very long time." Gently, he tilted her chin and pressed his lips to hers.

The kiss was tentative with restrained passion. Every cell in her body went still before sensation exploded throughout her nervous system. Jason was kissing her, and she was kissing him back.

His lips were cool and firm as they moved over hers, taking and giving all in one breath. She curled her fingers in his shirt to keep him close, not even realizing when she hooked a leg around his waist. He hoisted her up until his erection pressed to her heat.

God, he was thick and long. She grinded against him, sinking deeper into the kiss. He moaned into her mouth or was that her? She didn't care as long as he kept kissing her.

Jason pulled back, breathing hard. "You have an amazing mouth."

"So do you," she said with a breathless giggle. "No one has ever kissed me like that before."

He smiled, and she melted. GG became aware she was literally wrapped around Jason. Has she really thrown herself at him?

"Oh." She released her legs, but he held her dangling several inches off the floor.

"You didn't think it would be that easy to get away from me, did you?" he grinned.

She rested her head against his chest. "I don't want you to think I throw myself at anyone who kisses me senseless."

He allowed her to slide down his body but held her close once her feet met the floor.

"Oh, I know you don't." He cupped her butt.

Electricity crackled through her veins and drenched her panties. She was so turned on, she knew she'd have to break out her vibrator tonight. "I think I should leave."

"Too much heat in the kitchen?"

"Yes, but when I'm ready, I'll wear you out."

"Mmm, I love a challenge."

She raised on her tiptoes to kiss him. "Thanks for a great evening."

"Are you sure I can't persuade you to stay the night?"

"You can, but if I stay, neither of us will sleep."

Jason listened as GG's footsteps receded. The front door opened, then closed. He shifted his erection to a more comfortable position as he walked to the front door. He twisted the lock, then leaned against the wood. Learning GG had feelings for him, well maybe not so much feelings but chemistry, left him harder than frozen meat. He hadn't been lying when he told her she had an amazing mouth. He could imagine her lips and tongue swirling around his cock.

He groaned as his dick pulsed harder. Thinking like this was not going to help his raging hormones. He still had to figure out how to sleep with his cock on ten.

He shuffled toward the back of the house and his bedroom. He had no carpet, but either tile or laminate flooring. Slowly, he stripped off his clothes, dumping them in the hamper at his bedroom door. The phone rang.

"Call from August or Sol," the computerized voice announced.

Jason picked up the device, using a single digit to double tap the screen to answer. "Hello, love."

"Just calling to say goodnight," she said cheerfully. "Actually, I thought you'd be in bed by now."

"Likewise, my dear. Stx not putting you to bed right."

A distinct male voice, but the words unidentifiable, came through the line. Jason grinned; pretty sure he knew what August's love said. She chortled. "I'm not repeating that," she stated.

Jason laughed. "Let him know I'm teasing; I know he does right by you."

"He does," she agreed happily. "And I've only had to trip him once."

"Sounds fair. How about the three of you come by for Sunday dinner? I've got someone I'd like you to meet."

"Sure. Want me to bring anything?"

"Your appetites. I got everything."

⌒

The next morning, dressed in a fresh set of khakis and a dark blue polo shirt, Jason tied on an apron. He could shape the patties and make sure the seasoning was right with the meat before he set it aside for the casings. It was almost time to cold smoke another batch of brats. He also wanted to test out how the pickles would work with a new sandwich idea or, rather, a de-constructed sandwich idea. Jason also wanted to see how the flavor profiles of the pickles would work with the slaw, baked beans, and pulled pork.

He entered the large walk-in, grasped the handle of the utility cart, and rolled it out, maneuvering the cart to a nearby prep table.

Food was his life. Ever since he could remember, he'd been in the kitchen. His parents hadn't been the greatest of cooks, but they'd passed on their passion for food and trying new things to him. Some of his happiest memories were of him and his family in the kitchen. He usually was given some small task to do, like shelling nuts or peeling potatoes, and as he grew, he was pulling out the ingredients until he was finally preparing meals on his own.

He poured over cookbooks like most kids read bedtime stories. While his classmates learned their ABC's, he learned the difference between smothering and a fricassee.

He stowed the cart at his workstation, then went to retrieve the batch of pickles. As he lifted the gallon-size jar, the lid rattled. He paused. *Had I not closed it tight last night?* He paused long enough to reseal the lid and caught a whiff of something not quite right. Frowning, he carried the jar to his workstation, set it down, and unscrewed the lid. Garlic, dill, and a foul odor he couldn't identify wafted up from the jar. He dipped a finger in the jar and encountered a slimy substance. Well, that certainly wasn't right. *Had I somehow mixed oil with the pickle brine?* Not saying it couldn't happen, but if he'd been in a hurry . . . He lifted his fingers to his nose and sniffed. No, it didn't have the scent of oil. He tapped the tip of his tongue to taste the substance.

"Ugh!" He wiped his tongue on a nearby towel. Now that was just nasty for no reason. He walked to the end of the row until he reached a handwashing station. Quickly and thoroughly, he washed and dried his hands. Something wasn't right with the pickles. He replaced the lid and set the jar aside. Donning gloves, he opened the lid of the ground meat he'd made last night, scooped a few teaspoons out, and formed them into patties. He inhaled, but something sweet caught his attention. He wasn't sure if it was the bit of molasses he included or the mesquite.

He heated a skillet, added a bit of oil, and then tossed in the quarter-size patties. They cooked quickly and allowed them to cool slightly before he popped one into his mouth. There was that sickening sweet flavor and scent. It rolled around his tongue like rotten fruit, masking the salt, pepper, and other savory spices he added to the mix. Had he somehow gotten something rancid in the mix last night? If he had, the entire batch needed to be thrown away, and that was costly.

A door slammed. The soft fragrance of coconut and limes drifted in the air. Immediately, his body went on point—GG. All thoughts of rancid food fled at the remembered sweetness of her mouth and the heat of her body. He so could have easily had her on his kitchen counter last night if she'd let him.

They'd been willing, but she pumped the brakes.

"What's that smell?" she asked, striding toward him.

"The brats I made last night. I think one of the meats may have been rancid."

Keys jangled a moment before water ran. "I double-checked the dates. The meat was delivered and triple checked. I rejected the first delivery because it was too close to the expiration date."

They received fresh food deliveries every other day. If GG said the dates were correct, then they were correct. "And I think I mixed oil in the pickles instead of vinegar," Jason mentioned sheepishly. He could almost hear the frown in her voice.

"No," she drawled the word. "I made that brine."

The jar lid rattled again. "This isn't oil."

"Then what is it?"

"I don't know." She walked to the utility cart. "Are you trying something new in the brats?"

Jason paused in pulling out spices. "No. Why?"

"There's a bit of green rice in the mix."

Green rice? I didn't put any rice into the mix, let alone green rice.

"Oh God." She gasped.

He swung in her direction, alarmed at the note of stress in her voice. "What is it?"

"Did you eat any of this?" she demanded, her voice uncharacteristically shrill.

"Yeah. I always taste the batches until I get the seasoning where I want it."

Fabric moved. "Shit, I can't think."

"What is it?"

"Poison. Someone put poison in the meat. And you ate it."

Chapter Four

Ian positioned his food truck at his parking spot but did not immediately put the vehicle in park. He surveyed the parking lot. Several other food trucks lined the streets, but the spot reserved for The Dog Hut was conspicuously vacant. A small smile of satisfaction curved his lips.

That's right. If The Dog Hut didn't show, he could swing into the spot and easily double his sales for the day.

"I'll hop out and make sure we're lined up right." Dylan unhooked his seatbelt. When he didn't get a response, he looked at Ian. "Ian?"

"They're not here yet." Ian couldn't quite hide the glee from his voice.

Shrugging, Dylan slid out the door and then slammed it closed.

Ian stared through the windshield as Dylan made his way around the vehicle. If The Dog Hut vehicle didn't show up in the next five minutes, he could claim their spot. He glanced from his watch to the vacant area. Pounding on the back of the truck drew his attention to the driver's side mirror. Dylan was waving for him to back up.

With a huff, Ian jerked the shifter into R and left off the brake. He could at least pretend he was going to stay put. He couldn't allow Dylan to think anything had changed until things, well, changed. Dylan held up an open palm, and Ian stepped on the brakes again. He stared forward, and then silver and blue caught his peripheral. No, it couldn't be. The silver-and-blue truck, with a painted sign consisting of a barking brat on a bun inside a makeshift hut, parked in the vacant slot across from him.

"Fuck!" Ian swore. He slammed the shifter into park and turned off the engine with a savage twist.

"What's the hold-up?" Dylan demanded, opening the backdoor.

"Nothing," Ian grumbled.

"People are already lining up for the trucks."

"Whatever."

Dylan glanced over his shoulder as he donned an apron. "What bug died in your butt?" He pulled out a large pot filled with marinara. He would pair it with spaghetti squash or a cheese ravioli, both meatless and vegan.

When Ian got in the back of the truck, he slammed cabinets and drawers. What had he missed? He'd been pretty positive by tainting the food it would cost Jason today's assignment. He'd seen the prep for today's menu, and it should've taken Jason out of the game, unless they were selling the tainted food.

"I'll be right back." Ian patted his pocket, making sure he had his phone.

"Hey! We open in forty-five minutes!" Dylan called after him.

"This will only take a minute." As he disappeared out the door, Ian dialed the health department.

"I promise you I'm feeling all right," Jason assured the couple seated on either side of his hospital bed. Both of his visitors were blind: Samson, from a workplace accident and August from a degenerative eye condition, probably Retinitis Pigmentosa, as so many others in their group suffered.

"GG said you ate poison," August pointed out.

"Not a lot," Jason countered. A hand smacked his shoulder. "Ow."

"Use your words, Sol," Samson "Stx" Denver teased.

"I am using my words, but you men are hard-headed and stubborn," August snapped.

Jason caught August's hand between his. He hadn't wanted to worry her, but the only way he could get GG to work their spot today was to have August and Stx with him.

"Tell me what happened," Samson encouraged.

"The hospital is keeping me for observation. The fact we brought in samples with us helped speed up the process."

"But how did rat poison get into the food?" Stx wanted to know.

"Thank you for not accusing me of being blind and not knowing the difference between a box of d-con and rice."

"He better not," August snorted. "Considering he mixed up his shaving cream and whipped cream this morning."

"Whipped cream?" Jason prompted.

"We had splits," Stx supplied defensively.

"Kinky," Jason said.

August dissolved into a fit of giggles.

"Wait until I get you home, woman," Stx threatened good-naturedly. "I'm going to spank you."

"Don't threaten me with a good time," she retorted.

Jason grinned. Even if he couldn't participate at the moment, knowing August was happy filled him with happiness.

"Seriously, August, we need to know how this happened," Stx admonished.

"I don't know," Jason answered. "GG and I cleaned up last night. I prepped the meat for today as I planned to cold smoke a batch of brats. After GG and I went to dinner, I didn't step into the kitchen until this morning."

"Was anything disturbed?" Stx asked.

"Wait," August interrupted. "You and GG had dinner last night?"

"Sol!" Stx chided.

"Well, it's about time is all I'm sayin."

"About time?" Jason said.

Stx huffed his annoyance.

"Yes. You and GG have some sparks going on. You deserve more happiness in your life."

"Was anything disturbed?" Stx enunciated each word.

"Just so you know, Jason. I'm rolling my eyes."

Jason laughed. "All right." He sobered as he thought about what was or wasn't out of place. "The lid on the pickle jar wasn't tight. And now that I think about it, the lid on the meat mixture was upside down."

"And you and GG were the only ones in the prep area?"

"Alastair was there for a bit, but he had a class to get to so he took off early."

"Any way someone could get into the prep area without you knowing?"

"I'm sure there is, but I don't even keep rat poison anywhere on the premises. There's an exterminator who comes out like clockwork and checks everything. I've worked with the company for years." He shifted on the bed. "My company is so small; I can't afford a health inspector shutting us down for any type of violation. We always rate 'exceeds expectation.'"

"Do you have cameras on the place?"

"No," he answered. If he had, then he would know who had contaminated his food and tried to kill him.

"I'll call my son. He'll have cameras in your place by the end of the week," August said. She clicked her tongue. A dog came awake with a shake of tags. "Forward, find the door."

They waited until they could no longer hear the squeak of August's shoes on the linoleum or her voice, giving periodic commands to her guide dog.

"Do you know if there are cameras anywhere else in the neighborhood?"

"Probably." Jason adjusted the IV tube affixed to the back of his hand. "What scares me most isn't that I ate some of the poison, but if GG hadn't seen it, I'd have served it to my customers. Do you know how damaging that would've been to my business?"

"Yeah."

Jason sat back; he couldn't fathom anyone being angry or crazy enough to sabotage his business. There was more than enough property to share. Sure, the food truck market was ruthless, but it didn't warrant food poisoning.

"Any enemies?"

"No."

A knock sounded on the open door. "Evening, gentlemen. I'm Dr. Kronik." A deep-voiced man announced. "I have your lab results here."

"Wassup, doc?"

"Aside from the rat poison, we also found syrup of ipecac. Any idea how that got in your system as well?"

GG dragged a handkerchief over her face as she turned a batch of brats on the grill. The only reason she hadn't given their spot to another food truck was Jason was counting on her to keep going. She and Alastair were doing their best to get the orders out in a reasonable amount of time. However, without Jason manning the grill, it was a little harder. It didn't help knowing she was worried and would've preferred to stay with him instead of manning the truck.

"You sure Jason is good?" Alastair asked during a momentary lull.

She nodded. "They're keeping him overnight for observation."

"But how did someone get in? We don't even keep stuff like that on the premises." Alastair filled a couple of napkin dispensers before switching them out with the empty ones. There were still three tickets hanging in GG's window, and he had the buns prepped for the dogs, brats, and burgers.

"Did you notice anybody hanging around the house before you left yesterday?"

Alastair shook a basket of fries, then stopped the timer on them. He pulled the basket from the oil, shook off the excess before dumping the batch in a silver holding tray rimmed with salt. He sprinkled on a liberal amount, tossing the fries to ensure they were coated before portioning them between two cardboard trays. He wrapped the containers in wax paper before sliding them in a waiting paper bag. As he turned, GG was sliding the protein onto the appropriate buns. She wrapped and placed these in another paper bag. Before he could grab the ticket, she stapled it to the bag and handed it over. By the time he handed out the food, she had the last two orders put together.

"You're fast."

She flashed a smile. "Have to be if we want to stay number one."

That was the last bit of levity they had as they were slammed with another wave of hungry patrons. By the time they closed for the night, every scrap of food was gone; not even an errant bun or fry remained.

Tomorrow was only a prep day, so they didn't need to be anywhere. Not only would the day-off give them time to recoup the lost meat, but Jason would be in the kitchen. And him being in the kitchen reminded her of their shared moment the other day. Every time she brushed against Jason, she had the impression of an animal ready to pounce. And she was the prey. Maybe he hadn't been aware of the raw hunger on his face, but she'd seen it, reveled in it. The look was so potent and unadulterated, it left her panties damp and her body unfulfilled.

So, she kept brushing against him. As much as it flamed her desire, the brief contact also alleviated some of the ache.

And then they were busy, and there was no more time for teasing.

"Ready?"

GG looked around; Alistair made short work of the truck. Every surface was pristine and ready for the next go-round.

"Are you sure I can't help get something together?" He made sure all breakers were off before tossing the damp rag into an already overflowing laundry bag.

"Stop by in the morning. There will be plenty of work to do," she promised.

They parted ways at the driveway. GG dragged the laundry bag behind her as she fumbled for her keys. She eyed the lock on the garage door. The plate was fairly new, but there were scratches on the surface. She didn't remember those being there before.

Cautiously, she unlocked the door and stepped inside. Lights blazed to life. Since there was no food stuff to put away, she tossed the laundry in the washing machine, then went to grab the clipboard with tomorrow's production.

They would have to make up for yesterday's loss as well as have enough for tomorrow. *Had I remembered to call their meat vendor?* She pulled out her phone, scrolled through the call log, and sighed. Yes, she had. If they still didn't have enough, then she would go out and buy what was needed.

But now she had to know how Jason was doing. If she was honest, she needed to see Jason. Now that the day was at an end, her thoughts were consumed with him.

Of course, he texted her throughout the day, giving her updates. Probably the most disturbing was knowing the pickles had been contaminated. *Who was doing this?*

She walked into the freezer, shivering at the subzero temps, and quickly pulled out the items she would need for tomorrow. These she placed on a low shelf in the walk-in refrigerator.

Once more glance around the kitchen and she made sure nothing was out of place. She switched the laundry to the dryer, turned off the lights, and left the building. She double- checked the lock engaged as well as the deadbolt. It may not stop another break-in but it would slow the person down. She'd have to ask Jason about getting an alarm and cameras for the building.

Twenty minutes later, she was striding into U of M Hospital. The building covered several miles and seemed to be the heart of the city. *What if I hadn't seen the rat poison in the meat? How much of it would Jason have eaten before he succumbed to the toxin?* A cold wave of fear washed over her. She could've lost him.

And here she was thinking she had more time to pursue him, to bed him. No. Once Jason was released, she'd give him a serious welcome home. There would be no more delays on her end; she was going to know every inch of Jason Michaels. Last night had given her a taste of his potency and virility, and not acting on their shared chemistry made for a rough night of sleep. With her being so turned on, even the sheets caressing her naked flesh reminded her of Jason's hands.

She stepped into his room; no one else was present. He sat in a chair facing the window, commentary from a local news station drifted through the air.

"Hello GG," he greeted.

"How did you know it was me?" she quickly crossed the room.

"I just know."

He looked good, even in the blue hospital gown and bottoms. The robe wasn't hospital issue; it was smoky gray and super soft to the touch. The garments also revealed more of his tattoo. More flames disappeared into his collar. Again, she fought the urge to pull away the fabric and explore the source of the flames.

"I see August was here." She leaned down and pressed her lips to his. She poured relief and promise into her kiss. All the things she couldn't say went into the press of her lips.

Jason drew her to him, spilling her into his lap. She twined her fingers around the back of his neck and held him close.

"I'm so glad you're okay," she whispered, holding her cheek to his stubbled one.

He laughed a soft, rumbling sound, which vibrated through every cell in her body. She shifted on his lap, enjoying the erection poking her hip.

"If this is what it takes to get you on my lap, I should eat poison more often," he teased.

She wiggled her hips on his lap, and he groaned. "If you eat poison, I won't be able to welcome you home properly."

He placed his hands at her waist. "Baby, you're torturing me."

"Not staying the night tortured me. Knowing you were in the hospital today . . . If we hadn't been so busy today, I don't know what I would've done."

Jason kissed her slowly, tenderly, and with so much feeling, tears pricked her eyes. GG closed them soaking in the emotion. *Was this love or something else?*

"I see August stopped by," she whispered again against his lips.

"She and Stx are going to have someone drop by and install cameras and an alarm system to the house."

Relief surged through her. "Good. I wanted to suggest those things to you." She stroked her fingers over his head, enjoying the tight curls of his hair. "This may be nothing, but I noticed some scratches on the lock."

"I think if we talk to Sgt. Falls, he can really help with this."

"I don't want to be without you, Jason," GG blurted. "When you were injured, I feared I'd never see you again.

Knowing someone tried poisoning you and maybe even tried to kill you. I can't live without you in my life."

Jason placed a kiss on her lips. "We'll take this one day at a time; don't declare something from traumatic events."

"Are you saying you don't feel the same way?" she demanded, a note of hurt sliding through her.

"Baby, I'm in the hospital with you on my lap. I've a wicked hard-on and no way to alleviate it. If we were someplace less public, you'd be naked and I would be deep inside you, enjoying your heat and working on bringing you as much pleasure as possible."

GG sucked in a breath at his words. Not only did they soothe, but they aroused and stirred desires so potent she moved restlessly against him. She wanted to be naked and filled with him.

"I think there's a lock on the door," she managed huskily.

"No, baby. When I take you, I want to spend time getting to know your body." He traced a line of fire up her inner thigh.

She widened her stance to give him better access and cursed the fact she was wearing jeans. If she had on a skirt, he could touch her, slide his long, clever fingers inside her, circle her clit, and finger-fuck her. Instead, he stroked his fingers over the dampness of her crotch, as she pressed against his hand. If she moved just right, the pressure of his hand and the constriction of her jeans would give her a nice orgasm.

"Your scent is so intoxicating." He nuzzled her ear as he continued to stroke her. "I can't wait to have you on my tongue. To lick you like a tropical shaved ice and suck this," he circled her clit, "until I have all your cream in my mouth."

And just like that, her climax washed over her. Jason covered her mouth with his, swallowing her soft cries as she shuddered in his arms. She rested her forehead against his, breathing him in as she recovered her wits. No man had ever brought her climax so fast or with so little contact. "Wow."

"When I get home, I'll make it better for you," he promised.

Better? She might pass out from pure pleasure.

Chapter Five

The next afternoon, Jason stood at the buffalo chopper feeding chunks of lamb into the bowl. He stopped the machine, scooped a handful of the raw material for texture, dropped it back, and started the machine again. Across the way, GG was filling the casings for the hot dogs. On the other side of GG, Alistair chopped onions, garlic, and peppers. The scents combined and floated throughout the air. In fact, they should probably hit the exhaust fans, as the pungent aroma of onion was slowly overtaking the garlic and making his eyes water.

He stopped what he was doing, walked five paces to the wall, and used his elbow to flip the switch. Fans whirred to life.

He'd been released early that morning from the hospital, so now he was playing catch up. Today should've been spent cold smoking the brats, but now he'd have to finish them in batches. A knock reverberated through the room.

"I can't stop what I'm doing," GG called.

"Neither can I," Jason called back.

"I need a break," Alistair sniffled. He paused long enough to peel off his gloves, then blow and wipe his nose. "Damn onions are getting to me."

"Why do you think he turned on the fan?" GG retorted.

Jason laughed, returning his attention to his task. Once he had this batch ground, he placed it with a little pork and spices, and then let it sit overnight. Hopefully, no one would break in and contaminate this food again. One, he couldn't afford to replace the meat again; and two, he didn't relish spending another night in the hospital, having a tube shoved down his throat so they could give him charcoal to be certain the poison was pushed from his system.

"The, uh, health inspector is here," Alistair announced with an odd note in his voice.

Well, that was different. They weren't due for another inspection for another two months. "Give me just a sec to finish this," Jason said.

"I've got it," Alistair said, walking closer. He quickly washed his hands, donned gloves, and took over for Jason.

Jason did the reverse, peeling off his gloves and washing his hands. He also removed his apron, as he was pretty sure bits of food clung to it. The garment went into a laundry bag. He strolled in the direction of the squeaking shoes. "Hello. I don't think we've met." Jason held out his hand.

A plump, doughy hand grasped his. Jason had to fight the revulsion of the limp handshake; he'd filleted fish with more spine.

"Neelam Jones."

Even the voice spoke of bland limpness.

"What can I do for you, Mr. Jones?"

"We received a complaint you're serving tainted food," he explained. "Of course, we need to inspect your kitchen and the truck."

Behind him, movement ceased. Jason nodded. "I see." He swept a hand to encompass the kitchen. "Please do what you need to do."

"Your place is very organized and extremely clean," Jones stated.

Jason inclined his head. "We strive," he answered. "Would you like a tour, or would you prefer to wander?"

Both machines stopped; the sudden silence was jarring.

"I'm done here," GG said.

"I'll wander." The shoes squeaked away from Jason. "Your logs?"

"Next to the cooler."

"If you can't see, how do you keep track of temperatures?" Curiosity mixed within Jason as he tilted his head to the side, trying to decipher the tone. *Was it disdain or something else?*

Jason walked to the cooler, reached up, and pressed a button outlined in felt. "Temperature is 38 degrees Fahrenheit," a mechanical voice announced.

"I log the numbers into my phone, which adds them to a spreadsheet."

Fabric rustled. An awkward pause followed.

"Did you just nod?" Jason asked dryly.

Chuckles turned into coughs behind him, and Jason fought a smirk.

"Uh yeah. I did." Now embarrassment colored Jones's tone.

"No worries; it happens all the time."

"Excuse me," GG said, brushing against Jason.

The contact was subtle, no more than her behind brushing his wrist, but he felt the sing to every point in his anatomy. He cursed that he was no longer wearing an apron to hide the boner filling the front of his pants. He shifted, hoping his shirt covered the growing bulge.

A click, followed by a swirl of cold air, let Jason know GG was in the walk-in. Jason used the time to walk to where the clean aprons were kept, tied one on, and then donned a pair of prep gloves. He went back to his station, where Alistair had scooped the ground meat into a large mixing bowl.

"I think we're being set-up," Alistair whispered.

"I think you're right."

GG set the full container of hot dogs on a middle shelf. She'd already labeled the container and placed the appropriate braille lettering on the lid. She didn't like how quickly the health inspector showed up after the break-in and poisoning. This wasn't a coincidence; this was a clear attempt to try and shut them down.

If she hadn't turned over the tainted food to Sgt. Falls earlier, there would probably be a real issue. She rather liked the mature officer. He often volunteered with The Council of the Blind, an organization consisting primarily of the blind and visually impaired. The group often held get togethers, meetings, and more recently a "White Cane Awareness," which helped make the public aware of the purpose of a white cane and other mobility devices offered.

She scanned the walk-in, making sure nothing was out of place. Everything was labeled and dated.

However, GG noticed a package of carrots out of place and returned them to the other veggies. She turned to find Neelam watching her.

"I remember you," he stated.

She inclined her head.

"The restaurant doesn't run as efficiently. This cooler is more organized than anything I've ever seen." He touched a nearby food container with Tuesday's date. "Everything is labeled and dated per regulation."

"We strive for excellence."

He looked up, eyeing the fans and condenser for the fridge. "Even the blades and grates are clean."" He removed a thermometer from his pocket, wiped a disinfectant wipe along the tip before inserting it into a nearby tub of brats. "Anyone who has this type of cleanliness and organization should not have food complaints."

"Typically, we don't," she stated.

She left the fridge, followed by the inspector. He continued his tour around the kitchen, taking temps where needed and inspecting equipment before he finally stood beside the food truck. GG let him in, flipping the lights as they entered.

Every surface sparkled. He walked through the galley-style kitchen, opening doors and inspecting the fridge and fryers. He wrote something on his clipboard. "I'll be by the location tomorrow to watch you work."

GG nodded, flicked off the lights, and locked the door. She watched the inspector disappear down the drive before she hurried back into the prep kitchen.

Alistair was once again chopping onions, and Jason was back at the buffalo chopper. She watched him work, confident and at ease with his movements. She could almost forget he could no longer see; actually, she often forgot he could no longer see. Thoughtfully, she washed her hands, donned a fresh apron, and went back to work.

"What did he say?" Jason asked.

"He said he'd see us on site tomorrow." She switched out the tray for a clean one. Now she was going to load the casings for the brats.

Jason stood in the darkened living room. Work was over for the evening, and now it was time to relax. He didn't want to admit he was a little tired from the entire ordeal. The one thing they hadn't let him do in the hospital was sleep. Someone was in every five minutes it seemed to check on him. He hadn't had much of an appetite either. Slowly, he made his way to the sofa and sat. A sigh eased past his lips; this was one of those times he really didn't want to be alone.

The soft scuff of footsteps drew his attention toward the doorway. The scent of coconuts and limes tickled his nostril and tightened his groin. He wasn't alone.

"Everything is clean, locked and triple-checked for the night."

"Come." He patted the seat next to him. "Rest a bit."

GG sat next to him, her bare arm brushing his. Every cell in his body responded to the slight touch. He placed his arm around her shoulders, drawing her close. It seemed the most natural thing in the world for her to be here. "Now I can relax."

"Jason, we need to talk," she began.

"Should I be worried? We haven't even slept together yet," he teased.

She chuckled. "No, not like that. The whole thing with the inspector and the break-in."

"Cameras and alarm go in tomorrow. August has assured me her son will be gone before we return, but he'll come back by and show me how to operate the system."

She leaned her head on his shoulder, a hand pressed to his heart. "This just seems so personal."

He lowered his head until his nose brushed her hair. Definitely coconut. He turned into her, grazing her temple with his lips. Her skin held the citrusy zing of lime.

"You always smell so good." He kissed the corner of her eye, trailing minute kisses to the corner of her mouth.

She shifted as his lips played across hers while she settled more fully into the cushions. Jason tugged her shirt from the waistband of her jeans, trailing his fingers along her stomach and ribcage.

She wasn't skinny or fat; she was what the rappers and other urban artists considered thick, with all womanly curves and softness. He palmed one lace-covered breast as he swallowed her soft moans. Their tongues dueled, and all he could think of was this was not enough.

GG cupped the back of his head while he suckled her nipple through the fabric of her shirt. She arched her back, wishing the confines of clothing was not between them. She needed skin-to-skin contact.

"Jason," she whispered, once her mouth was free.

"Is that a plea for me to stop?" he asked huskily.

"No. If you don't let me outta these clothes, I'm gonna combust."

He laughed, and it sifted over her like fine sugar. "Yes, let's get out of these clothes."

There was a flurry of movement, clothing rustling and the soft thud of fabric as it hit the floor. Jason ran his palms up and down GG's softness, learning her dips and valleys. Wherever his hands touched, his mouth followed. Her scent beckoned, and he worked his way between her thighs.

"I've dreamt of tasting you for so long," he murmured. He slid one long digit from her clit to her slick heat. Her hips rocked at the movement, and he repeated the motion. He pried her lush lips apart and swept his tongue inside.

A whimper reached his ears, and a wave of satisfaction rolled over him. He always enjoyed pleasuring women, but this woman meant more to him. He wanted, no needed, to see to her pleasure. He wanted to make sure she would be his, and his alone.

"Oh God, Jason," she moaned.

She squirmed beneath his marauding mouth, and he cupped her buttocks, keeping her close. He didn't want to waste a drop of her sweet cream or miss a shudder of her tantalizing skin.

GG gripped the sofa cushions; never in her life had she had a man eat her out like Jason was doing. Tension coiled, winding her tighter and tighter. As if sensing this, he backed off, sucking her clit and teased it with barely there licks. She wanted to scream at him to let her cum, but no words left her lips or so she thought.

"I will, baby," he promised. "Let me love you tonight." He slipped two fingers inside, moving in and out like she wanted his cock to do. He kept the strokes lazy while he flitted his tongue over the sensitive bundle of nerves.

GG grounded against his mouth, hoping to relieve the ache, but his strong hand held her in place. Over and over, he teased, building her desire and backing off until she was panting with need. Only then did he slip a third finger inside her, pressed up and bit her clit. She shattered in his arms. Before she finished her climax, he was moving over her, filling her with his thickness. He was large, larger than any of her previous lovers, but he slid home as if he was made for her.

"Don't stop," she pleaded.

"Not on your life."

Slowly he withdrew, her tight muscles gripped him, unwilling to release their prize. When he slammed home, pleasure demanded he do it again. The slap of flesh on flesh as well as the rhythmic creak of the furniture provided the background music of their lovemaking. GG wrapped her legs around Jason's waist, locking her ankles at the small of his back. He slid a few more millimeters inside, and she gave herself over to them. She caressed his back, kissed his lips, and nibbled on the underside of his jaw as he pounded into her. Another wave of ecstasy rippled over and, through her, building with the promised pressure of a major release.

"Cum for me," he murmured against her lips. He grounded against her already sensitive clit. With his hard, easy strokes, she flew apart, and the only thing keeping her anchored in reality was their intimate joining. Jason dropped his head in the hollow of her shoulder as he embraced his own orgasm.

They laid there intertwined, panting and sweaty. She drifted her fingers over the taut muscles in his back and shoulders.

"Did I hurt you?" he asked softly.

"Mmm."

He chuckled. "Was that a yes or no?" He shifted until she was sprawled across him.

Cool air skittered across her bare buttocks, making her shiver. Jason pulled a knitted throw from the back of the sofa and draped it over them.

"Wow." She traced the ring around his nipple.

"I can say the same thing about you."

She pillowed her head on her hands as she gazed into his face. A satisfied smile creased his full lips, and he seemed much more relaxed than he had in a long time. An unfamiliar emotion squeezed her heart and flowed through her. She wanted to wake up to this man every chance she got. Her gaze landed on the ink trailing over one pectoral: the rest disappearing beneath his right arm. She traced the scales of the dragon, as the ink was so intricate the skin seemed to come alive beneath her fingertips.

"What is it?"

"I finally get to see your tattoo." She couldn't keep the awe out of her voice.

His chuckle rumbled through her. "Is that all?"

"All I could see were the flames peeking out of your collar but never knew what it was to."

"You could've asked." He stroked her butt.

"This is much better." She kissed the ink grazing his nipple. His hand tightened on her ass. "Ready for more?"

"What were you really thinking?" he prodded.

She kissed him. "I think I'm in love with you."

Chapter Six

Utter and total chaos. GG stared at the throng of people outside the food truck. There was no way they could accommodate all of these hungry people. She glanced at the clock above the order window. They still had fifteen minutes before they officially opened. She snuck a glance at Jason behind the grill. For someone who hadn't gotten much sleep last night, he was fresh and jovial.

She shifted, wincing a little at the soreness. There were whisker burns in places she never thought possible. A secret smile flitted over her mouth as she recalled exactly how she got those whisker burns.

"Earth to GG." Alistair waved a hand in front of her face. "Are you with us?"

She blinked, bringing Alistair's grinning face into focus. "Uh, what'd I miss?"

"Start taking orders so we can start moving product." He sidled back to his workstation, where packages of hamburger and hot dog buns waited for their grilled counterparts.

"You seem far away," Alistair said. "Did you have a hot date last night?"

Heat crept into her cheeks, and she was glad Alistair couldn't see the flush. "You could say that."

"Anybody I know?"

GG cast a glance at Jason, who burst out laughing.

Alistair stared between the two of them. "Did I miss something?"

"Look alive," she said, watching the inspector weave his way through the crowd. "Company's coming."

"How are they still operating?" Ian demanded. He glared out the takeout window to the silver-and-blue food truck across the way. He counted the crowd clustered in front of the truck, then compared it to the group in front of his. Well, he had more people; that made him feel a little better.

"How is who open?" Dylan asked, stirring a pot of marinara.

"Nothing," he mumbled, taking another order. He placed the ticket on the rack.

"We might want to double-check our security. I heard The Dog Hut was vandalized."

"Oh?"

"Yeah. My sister works in the emergency room at the U of M, and she mentioned how one of the employees was poisoned."

"That's messed up." Ian turned so Dylan wouldn't see the smile.

Dylan ladled the thick, rich, fragrant sauce into 10 oz. foam cups and applied the lids before packing them in a waiting bag. He tossed in the waiting utensils, napkins, and breadsticks.

Ian gathered the order and three more bags before he set it on the counter.

"We definitely don't want the same thing to happen to us."

"I doubt anything will happen to us." Ian waved toward a trio of customers. He handed out the bags, then stared at the inspector walking into The Dog Hut. There had to be something he could do to sabotage Jason's food truck.

"I've got an order for three of those cauliflower crust pizzas," Dylan said.

Ian nodded. He walked to a small cooler, pulled out three crust shells, and placed them on a baking stone. His gaze roved around the interior of the truck for any type of inspiration for sabotage. All he had handy were large containers of herbs and spices and raw sugar. He ladled pizza sauce on the crusts and added handfuls of shredded mozzarella cheese before tossing toppings haphazardly on the cheese. He smiled as he caught sight of a round container. Just what he needed. Quickly, he shoved the pizzas in the oven and grabbed a container of salt. "Be right back."

"Hey!" Dylan cried. "We're swamped!"

Ian slammed the door while leaving the truck, glancing right and left before darting behind the truck, then around another food truck. He had to make this quick or else he'd be noticed. The generator for The Dog Hut wasn't far. As a matter of fact, it was partially hidden between two other food trucks and a couple of grills. He meandered toward the big engine, unscrewed the gas cap, and dumped in the salt. Quickly, he replaced the cap and slunk back the same way.

As Ian neared the crowd at his truck, he dropped the salt in one of the pockets of his apron. Pretending he hadn't just wreaked havoc on a rival, he pulled out his order pad and mingled with his crowd.

The odor of something metallic burning drifted to Jason, and he sniffed the air. Carefully, he slid a hand along the edge of the grill, making sure he hadn't left a utensil or other non-cookable item on the grill. It wouldn't be the first time, but he certainly didn't want to do it in front of the health inspector.

Faint scratching also reached Jason's ears; *the inspector must be writing again*, he thought. To his credit, Mr. Jones stayed out of the way as much as was possible in the small confines, which Jason appreciated. Suddenly, a hiss and sputter drew his attention to the generator outside. Was it his or someone else's?

"Got in four large orders for twelve bacon burgers, six cheddar dogs, and eighteen brats," GG sidled next to him.

"That's three orders," Jason responded.

"No. That's the first large order. Do we have enough to fill it before I begin on the rest?"

"Who are they feeding, the football team?" Alistair quipped.

Jason barked his laugh. "What are the other orders?"

She rattled them off.

"We can do it, but we're done for the day," Jason told her.

"Cool."

As she turned to go back to the counter, silence, other than the hissing of meat on the grill, filled the air.

"Sounds like you're out of fuel,'" the health inspector commented.

Losing the generator now wouldn't be a huge thing, more of an inconvenience as it would force them to run the truck. He preferred using the generator, but he also needed running water. The health inspector would not allow them to continue serving if they didn't have a means of washing their hands. He wasn't too concerned about the grill, as he utilized a combination of wood and propane to cook.

"I'll check it," Alistair volunteered. "Keep the orders going."

Tension seeped through the truck, so Jason merely reached in the nearby fridge for the patties and dogs he needed.

"Does anything ruffle you?" the inspector asked.

"Sure, but we've planned for this." After he laid down the raw meat, he stripped off the soiled gloves, washed his hands, and donned a fresh pair.

GG walked to the front of the truck and hit a button. "That should hold us until we get the generator started, or we're done with these last few orders," she announced to them.

Alistair returned and the door slammed behind him. "Not sure what's going on with the fuel. The tank is at 3/4; it seems like there's something blocking the intake or outflow." He quickly washed his hands, donned a clean apron and gloves, and resumed putting together the sandwiches.

"It seems like you have everything in hand. Even with this turn of events, you're still up to code."

"Thanks," Jason called to Mr. Jones.

"It has been my pleasure to observe someone who takes food safety as serious as you do. Keep up the good work," Mr. Jones said and then left the truck.

For a long moment, no one spoke after the inspector left. As meat was done and removed from the grill, Jason added more.

An hour later, with the last of the orders completed and the takeout window closed, they began cleaning up for the day.

"So, nobody's going to address the alligator in the truck?" Alistair demanded.

"We got through it," GG said wearily. "That's all that matters."

"Someone is trying to put us out of business," Alistair stated.

"Maybe the hotel is trying to get GG back," Jason tossed out.

GG snorted. "They don't want to pay me what I'm worth. Besides, this is personal."

"So, who has it out for The Dog Hut?"

"That's a very good question. Maybe we should ask some of the people still milling around if they saw anything," Jason suggested. "I did smell something burning before the generator went down."

"I didn't smell anything," Alistair denied.

"Me either," GG stated.

"If I'm not mistaken, it's still under warranty," Alistair said. "I'll call and have someone come out and look at it."

"C'mon. Let's get done so we can all go home."

—

"So, this is the keypad," DJ Williams explained. "I placed tiny bump dots on the arm/disarm button. There's a square dot on the panic button. Is there any other buttons you'd like me to identify for you?"

Jason smiled. "This is good, especially since the five is already notched."

"Right. May I have your phone?"

"For what?"

"So, I can sync the system with your phone. This way you can check who's at the door when you're away or anywhere in the house. It will also allow for geofencing."

"Geofencing?" GG asked.

"Instead of using the keypad to enter, his phone will send a signal to unlock the door."

Jason handed over the device. When it announced the time, Jason held out his hand. "I can turn off the accessibility feature for you."

"I got it," DJ said. "My mom does the same thing. Most times I can work with it on, but for this, we'll work with it off and then I'll turn it back on so you can get used to the system."

"You did all this work while we were out," GG marveled.

He tossed her a smile. "When Mom pulls the mother card, you do what she says."

Jason laughed. "I appreciate this."

"Yeah. No problem."

Thirty-eight minutes later, Jason and GG were alone in the house. "This is so cool," GG said, looking over Jason's shoulder to the phone in his hand. They sat on the sofa in his living room.

Jason enjoyed the soft weight of GG's breast pressed against his back. Her scent curled around him, hardening his cock. Sharing little moments like these with her was something he could really get used to.

"You can see the entire property inside and out," she stated.

"And since it records directly to the cloud, I don't need to worry about changing discs or anything like that." Jason set down his phone and turned to draw GG into his arms. She came willingly and settled in his lap, as if she spent every available moment there.

"I don't think I will ever get enough of you," he murmured against her lips.

"Only because this is new," she retorted, sliding her fingers beneath his shirt.

He sighed, relishing her touch. He held her, breathing her in and enjoying the softness of her derriere rubbing against his hard cock.

"Maybe," he conceded. "But I'd like to think we've had chemistry for a long time now." He trailed kisses over her lips, cheeks, and eyes before returning to her mouth. He took his time once more, learning the taste and texture of her, indulging his senses until only their heavy breathing could be heard. He palmed her breast through her shirt, strumming the tight nipple until she moaned and pushed into his palm.

He wanted her wild against him, so he continued to pinch and tease her nipples, alternating between breasts. He tugged up her shirt, pulled down her bra, and laved the tight bud with his tongue.

She shifted until she straddled his thighs, her heat grinding against his hardness.

Her shirt and bra were no longer barriers, as Jason squeezed one pert boob and he licked the other. Her scent, heady and all female, beckoned him to continue, so with his free hand, he grabbed a handful of her ass and held her close.

GG gave herself over to sensation. Their first time, she thought, could've been a fluke; after all, it had been a while since she'd gotten laid. But something about the way Jason touched her body, as if he knew which cords to stroke, sent her libido into overdrive. So she'd taken to the habit of keeping more than one pair of panties in her purse because whenever they were in the same room, or she thought about him too long, her crotch was drenched. There was something about this man that drove her wild, and all she wanted to do was spend her free time naked and beneath him, or on her knees, or riding him.

She worked his belt and pants loose until she could grasp the long, thick length of him. He was so big, such a contradiction of steel-encased velvet. She stroked him up and down, rubbing her thumb over the head of his penis. She wanted to taste him to see if she could make him lose control.

GG slid off his lap, kneeling between his legs. Before he could protest, she licked the head of his cock. The spicy taste of male burst across her tongue, and she craved more. She sucked him with her mouth, and his fingers tightened in her hair. She sucked, alternating between hard and soft, slow and fast, until he thrust in time with her strokes.

Jason reveled in her mouth. Hot, tight, and, oh God, she knew how to use that tongue. If she kept going, he was gonna bust a nut down her pretty throat. *Was she ready for that? Could she take it?*

"GG?" he murmured.

"Hmm?"

"You're gonna make me cum."

A soft chuckle vibrated through his cock and his balls tightened. The climax seemed to tingle in his toes, race up his calves, and pool right there in his lap. His hoarse cry echoed off the ceiling, as she continued to suck and lick until he was only a quavering mass.

"You've got me so wet." She drew his hand to her pussy.

"Trust me, I'm going to make you wetter," he promised, stroking those dewy folds.

Chapter Seven

Ian and David surveyed the ranch-style house, as David adjusted the duffle slung over his shoulder.

"You sure you wanna go through with this?" David nodded at the hulking food truck. "I can make it look like negligence."

Ian twirled the crowbar he held. "Of course, I want to do this. I would think you'd want to do this since he's also sleeping with the woman you love."

White teeth flashed in the darkness. "I already have something significant planned for them. I didn't break out of prison just to sit back and watch her be happy." For a moment, David stood lost in thought. He'd planned out every bomb in order to garner August's attention and force her to fall in love with him. All his machinations had earned him were a dead sister and a prison sentence. And August still ended up with the man David tried to kill.

Ian wedged the thin end of the crowbar into the seam between the lock and the sill and pried hard. The door to the food truck popped open with a snap of wood. David grabbed the door before it could hit the side of the truck.

"Do whatever it is you do," Ian whispered over his shoulder. "I'll take care of the equipment inside." He disappeared into the darkness. The stainless-steel surfaces gleamed in the faint moonlight. He had to stand a moment and survey the space. He opened cabinets and drawers, finding only clean utensils, takeout containers, and a few cleaning supplies. *How could a single blind man manage all of this?* He had full sight, and his space wasn't this clean. He ran a finger over the grill grates; not even a speck of grease or char could be found.

For the space of three heartbeats, Ian doubted what he was about to do. How would he feel if someone came along and destroyed all he worked hard making a name and reputation for? And Ian had worked hard for his food truck. When vegetarian and vegan foods weren't the rage, he staked his name and reputation on tasty food without the meat. He removed the can of spray paint from the backpack, and here he was, destroying someone else's dream.

A sigh rushed past his lips, as he realized he couldn't do it. It was one thing to possibly sicken people, sabotage the generator, and call the health inspector, but seeing these gleaming surfaces, the license on the wall, he couldn't vandalize The Dog Hut. The amount of care and love oozed from every surface.

David appeared in the truck's doorway. "Let's go, snowflake."

Ian didn't need to be told twice. "After this, we go our separate ways," he said, hustling down the driveway.

"Fine by me.

With one last glance over his shoulder, Ian almost wished he could take back what he'd already set in motion. At least he wasn't the one who actually destroyed the truck.

The consoling thought fell flat, and Ian prayed he would get away with it.

The ballroom was happy, loud, and filled with the scent of expensive perfumes, aftershaves, and oily politicians. Jason wheeled his cart, loaded with a heat lamp and a rib roast to yet another table. The occupants of this table oohed and ahhed at the presentation. He offered a bright smile, knowing how he looked in his chef's white and the tall toque, the name for the chef's hat on his head. He loved his job. The best thing in life was feeding people, and he was good at it. Everywhere he looked, someone was enjoying the food he prepared.

He glanced over, spying GG in her more-fitted chef's coat and black slacks. Her dark hair was pulled into a bun at the nape of her neck. A hairnet and a floppy chef's hat kept the look professional, but she was still beautiful.

He had a rule though: he didn't date co-workers or subordinates. But looking at GG, he wanted to break all of his rules and make her one of his loves. He paused in slicing a section of medium rare steak. *Would GG be open to his lifestyle?* He knew no other way to live. Having multiple loves fulfilled him and made him whole and complete. *He wanted GG as a part of his life, but would she be willing?*

A tinkle of glass sounded out, and something dropped on his shoulder. He glanced at a bit of sparkle against his jacket. A loud crack drew his attention upward, as the chandelier came hurtling toward him. He didn't have time to jump out the way and couldn't have even if he tried. The table's occupants were shoving and screaming in their panic to flee, but he could only stare at the inevitable.

Crash!

Jason sat bolt upright, clamping his hands to his face. He'd expected the sticky hot wetness of blood and pain but found only sweat. He sucked in a lungful of air but tasted ash and fuel.

"What was that?" GG demanded, sitting beside him.

Jason grasped her hand. He wasn't in the ballroom where he'd lost his vision, but in bed with GG. However, from somewhere, another crash and crackle could be heard.

"Oh, my God!" GG scrambled over him out of the bed.

"What is it?" he demanded, following her hurried footsteps.

"The truck is on fire!"

Chapter Eight

"We came as soon as we could Uber," August stated, wrapping an arm around Jason and GG. "I'm so glad neither of you were hurt."

GG accepted the hug as she wiped her tears away. "Who would do this?" She turned to Jason, wrapping an arm around his waist. "Nothing was left on."

"I know," Jason said solemnly. He couldn't quite make sense of the loss. Sure, the insurance would cover this, but this was too close to home, way too close for comfort. Someone stepped onto his property and effectively put him out of business for the foreseeable future.

They stood inside the only garage bay with a working door. It was empty, as he didn't own a vehicle and the other half of the dwelling had been converted to a commercial kitchen.

"The fire marshal is definitely saying it was arson," Samson spoke up.

"I wish we knew who was doing this," GG lamented.

Jason stood straighter. "We do."

"What?"

"DJ installed the cameras today." Jason pulled out his phone. "He walked me through everything. I just need to find the right timeframe."

"The kid is the best!" Samson announced with pride.

"That's great!" August exclaimed. "GG can identify the person."

"If I can," GG capitulated. She peered over Jason's arm. "How far back should I go?"

"Try an hour before we called 9-1-1," she suggested.

Jason manipulated the phone. The speech was so fast, but he barely paid attention to the voice.

"Stop!" GG said.

Warm fingers surrounded his as the phone was tilted more in her direction. "There's two of them." She held his hand. "I recognize the guy going into the truck, but not the other one."

Ian grinned from ear to ear as he drove his food truck into the parking lot of the microbrewery. This morning, he'd received a phone call from the owner stating he would have the prime spot right outside the main entrance. And not only did he have that prime spot instead of the rear entrance, but he would also have the entire weekend as long as the brewery was open. That was a boon, as the brewery saw the majority of their patrons from Thursdays to Sundays. And Ian would be there for the duration.

"Did they say why we're getting the front?" Dylan stifled a wide yawn. "Personally, I think we make more money at the rear entrance than the front."

"But everybody will see our food truck," Ian pointed out.

"I guess. So, what happened to The Dog Hut?"

Ian shrugged. "Dunno," he lied. He parked the truck in the diagonal and turned off the motor. "We're here; they're not. It's as simple as that."

They weren't through with their setup before hungry patrons formed a line. The rich scent of savory red sauce and a creamy alfredo simmered on the induction eyes. Dylan opened and closed drawers and cabinets, a frown on his face.

"What's your boggle?" Ian asked, drawing curly cues and ivy on a chalkboard.

"Salt." He lifted a round container. "I remember putting two brand-new containers in here, and now there's only one."

Ian froze. He'd forgotten to replace the salt he used to sabotage the generator. "You sure?"

Dylan shot him a glare. "Of course, I'm sure; I marked it on the sheet." He waved a hand to the laminated inventory sheet taped to the outside of the cabinet door. "I double-check the inventory before we leave for the day."

"Don't worry about it." Ian checked his watch. "We've got time to run and grab some more."

⌒

"It looks a lot worse in the sunlight," GG commented.

Jason laid a careful hand on the charred, twisted metal. Some areas were still warm to the touch. "The insurance adjuster said it's a total loss."

"Are you sure Ian is the one who did this?" Alistair asked from Jason's other side.

They all stood in the brisk October air outside Jason's Ann Arbor home. A flatbed truck had yet to arrive to remove the vehicle.

"Yeah." Jason's tone was flat.

"You think maybe he did some of the other things, like poisoning you and the health inspector?"

"The cops aren't sharing too much, but I believe he's behind it all," Jason answered. "I wish I knew why."

"Jealousy," GG snapped.

"What?"

"Our truck has been more successful and visible than his," GG surmised.

"That's ridiculous," Jason argued. "What The Dog Hut does and I, Dyne does is like comparing apples to oranges. I feed the carnivores, and he goes after the tree-huggers."

Alistair released a low whistle. "It's a good thing you had cameras installed. You may have never found out who was doing this."

"We still don't know the second man on the video," Jason stated. He trailed fingers down GG's back; he couldn't resist. The entire loss of his business, no matter how temporary, had him seeking her comfort.

"Is something going on between you two?" Alistair demanded. "I've noticed y'all keep sending each other goo-goo eyes."

"I do not make goo-goo eyes," Jason protested.

"You do," Alistair included a laugh in his voice. "I think it's great if the two of you are finally hooking up."

"What do you mean by that?" GG demanded, planting her hands on her hips.

Now Alistair was outright laughing. "It means you two make a great couple, and I'm happy for you."

Snickering, Jason drew GG against him. "Forget it, love; we've been found out."

Later in the day, GG watched Jason move around the house. The short-sleeve shirt and sweatpants accentuated his muscles rather than covered them up. Resting her chin in hand, she released a contented sigh. He was such a beautiful specimen of man, and he was hers.

"You're thinking about me," Jason teased.

"Am not," she denied automatically.

He laughed.

"Well maybe a little bit."

"What about?" He moved into the kitchen opening cabinets, removing various items and setting them on the counter.

"What does this mean for us? I mean, where will I fit into your life along with August?"

Jason paused, an open bag of grits in his hand. "I've given that quite a bit of thought."

Something akin to panic and fear tightened in GG's belly. She didn't want him to discard her so early in their relationship, but she didn't want him to end what could be a real long-term, committed relationship. She rather liked the idea of not being the sole person in charge of his happiness. Besides that, she liked August. GG, herself, might not want to date other men, but she definitely wanted to be Jason's.

"I was thinking of asking you to be my partner." He set down the grits and walked to where she sat. "This is a huge step for me because I've never asked another woman to live with me, or we can go back and forth if that suits you better."

GG nearly slid off her stool. *Did he really just ask me to move in with him?* "You want me to move in with you?" she asked quietly, not quite trusting what she'd heard.

He offered her a wide smile. "Of course. You are one of the few women I want to share my life with. It may not be a traditional relationship, but I will treat you with all the love, respect, and admiration you deserve."

GG swallowed the lump in her throat.

He came around the counter and took her hands in his. "I love you, Greta. I have for a long time. I'm sorry I didn't act on it before now."

She giggled through her tears. "You're only saying that because you lost your food truck."

He caressed her cheek, and she leaned into his palm. "I'm really glad I didn't lose you. My life and career would be bleak without you in it."

She cupped his face between her palms and placed her lips on his in a soft, promising kiss. "I love you too."

Ian couldn't believe his good fortune; they were making money hand over fist. Twice now he had to send someone out for more ingredients to make certain dishes, but for the most part, they'd been able to keep up with the demand. He paused long enough to wipe his face with a napkin as he glanced at the clock. This was only the lunch rush; what were they in for during the evening festivities?

He looked over at Dylan, who was concentrating on making another pot of marinara. "Isn't this great?" he gushed.

"Definitely busy," he stated. "When is help arriving? I can't keep up the orders and cook."

"Sure you can," Ian encouraged. "Are you behind right now? I've a lull in orders."

Dylan shook his head. "I got it."

Ian frowned. "What's the matter? I thought you'd be thrilled at the profit we're making."

A knock on the side of the truck dragged their attention to the window. Two men with hard flat eyes stared back at them. A trickle of fear slid down Ian's spine.

Play it cool, Ian told himself, as he plastered a genial smile on his face. "What can I do for you?"

"We're looking for Ian Brown," the older one said.

"I'm Ian." He couldn't keep the fear from sliding into his voice. Sweat beaded on his forehead, and it had nothing to do with the heat in the truck.

"I'm Sergeant Falls, and this is my partner, Detective Potter. Would you mind stepping out of the truck so we can speak with you?"

Ian swallowed hard and glanced at Dylan. His partner goggled at him, puzzlement and confusion written in every line of his face. Ian turned back to the window, his mind racing. What was he going to do? He couldn't run, as running would only make him guiltier than he already was.

"Can it wait?" he tried. "We're really busy right now, and I can't leave my partner short- handed."

The officers glanced at one another, a silent message passing between them. "Sure. We've got time to kill."

"What's that about?" Dylan asked Ian, as they assembled their first three orders.

Ian shook his head, not trusting his voice. *How am I going to get out of this?* He looked from the two officers to the back door to Dylan and back again. "I'm sorry, Dylan."

"What?" He stapled the bags closed before starting on three more orders.

As Ian handed out the last order, Sgt. Falls stepped into the cramped space holding two things, a piece of paper and a pair of handcuffs.

"You're being arrested?!?" Dylan squeaked.

Ian trembled as he stared at the stainless-steel restraints. "I-I," he stammered, then fell silent. He hung his head as the steel snapped around his wrists. Det. Potter recited Ian's Miranda rights from a small card he held as Ian was propelled from the food truck. All Ian knew was what he'd done wasn't worth the trouble he was in now.

Chapter Nine

"He confessed to everything." Jason held GG in his arms. They laid on the couch as some rom-com movie provided background noise. As Adam Sandler's character wailed, "Pretty, pretty please," Jason grinned. He loved *The Wedding Singer*.

"He confessed."

Jason nodded. "Before they could book him, he was already telling Sgt. Falls and Det. Potter what he'd done. Everything from breaking into the kitchen to adding rat poison and ipecac syrup to the food, salt in the generator, and breaking into the truck the other night to set it on fire."

"Why would he do all this?" GG answered incredulously.

"From what Sgt. Falls surmised, Ian was jealous at the attention our truck received. He thought I received special treatment because I'm blind."

"Well, that's just nonsense!" she scoffed. "I mean I know I floated the idea of him being jealous, but you worked hard to build your reputation, not only as a chef but as a food truck operator."

He smoothed a hand over her hair, then down her spine to cup her butt. God, he loved the way this woman felt; all soft curves and she loved him for him. When others had fled because of his accident, GG stayed, offering support and friendship. She didn't even baby him as others tended to do with overhelping, which drove him crazy. He knew how to sit in a chair or fasten his seatbelt. There was no need for these over helpful people to put their hands on his hips to guide him down into a chair or to even assist him in the bathroom. God, even blind, he knew how to point and aim. At least, GG waited until he asked for help before offering.

"He signed a confession to that extent." He brushed a kiss along the curve of her cheek.

"Have you given any thought as to what we're going to do for the rest of the week? We've got an event we're supposed to cater this weekend." She nuzzled his hand as she wiggled against his rising erection.

Jason pressed her more firmly against him as he thrust up. There was no way he was going to let her get away with teasing him like this. "We've got the back-up truck."

She wrinkled her nose. "That thing is one good bump from falling apart."

"You're wrinkling your nose at me."

"How you know that?"

She waved her hand in front of his face.

The breeze she created fanned her scent of coconut and lime to him. He grabbed her wrist and pressed a kiss to the center of her palm. "Your voice goes all squeaky, like when you scrunch your face. And the other truck isn't that bad; it will get us through until we get the replacement."

She slid off him, tugging at his hand.

"I thought we were fooling around." He allowed her to pull him to his feet.

"Yes, but I want to start and finish this in the bedroom."

He held her close, pushing her back against a nearby wall. "I like being able to take you when and where I like." He brought his mouth down on hers.

She ringed her arms around his neck, hooking a leg at his waist. He hoisted her until she settled over his erection.

"You drive me crazy," she said, between kisses. Somehow, he'd worked her out of her clothes, his hands sliding over her skin to imprint her texture and smoothness on his senses. GG moaned her pleasure and squirmed against him.

Jason inhaled deeply, her scent beckoning and intoxicating. He needed to be inside her. He grasped the base of his cock, using the head to tease her clit, which was already slick and wet for him. He didn't think but drove deep. Only the slightest resistance met his stroke. Another push, and he was sheathed deep. Her muscles gripped and massaged him, welcoming him home.

"Hold tight, baby; this is going to be a little rough," he promised.

GG met him stroke for stroke, and she loved it. She tried to move, but his large hands kept her in place for his upward thrusts. His mouth dominated hers, as every kiss, every stroke, branded her as his. The connection was so potent between them that she felt it in her very soul. She dug her fingers into the hard muscles of his shoulders and allowed her orgasm to take her under. Fire raced and danced along sensitive nerve endings, and still, he didn't not allow her a release. He always seemed to know when she was close and backed off just enough to keep her teetering on the edge. After the third time, she nipped his ear lobe. "Stop teasing me and let me cum," she begged.

He chuckled and retaliated by biting her nipple, which only bathed his cock in her warm heat. He scraped her clit, sinking deeper with each thrust. Tension built and coiled so tight, GG was sure her heart would stop.

Jason swirled his tongue around the hard bud of her nipple as he ground against her. So deep and filled with sensation, she exploded. Sound and sight evaporated until only feeling was left, and she was flooded with such intense pleasure that one orgasm rolled right into another. When he came, the hot, jerky spurts of his climax ignited another one in her.

"Oh," was all she managed to say. He collapsed over her, and she realized they were no longer in the hall against a wall. How the hell had they got to his bedroom?

"When did we get here?" she murmured.

He chuckled. "On your knees," he prompted.

"You can't possibly."

His very eager cock nudged her hip.

She rolled to her knees.

"Oh, I think I can."

Chapter Ten

August clutched Samson's hand. "Are you sure?"

"We're very sure," Sgt. Falls answered.

Samson drew August closer, holding her tight. He hated the trembling in her body, knowing it was from fear as much as anxiety. "I thought he'd been picked up already. With Rodney and the other guy," Samson stated.

Sgt. Falls shifted on the sofa. "We did that so we could flush him out."

"David Foster has been out this entire time?" August demanded, enunciating each word. "The man who assaulted me outside my place of work, then sent bombs to me? That David Foster?" Her voice had risen, so Samson squeezed her hand.

"Sol," he began in a consoling voice.

"If you tell me to calm down, I'll hide your cane," she threatened. "That mad man tried to kill us! Not to mention he's the reason you're blind."

"August, please," Sgt. Falls soothed. "We've had your home and work under surveillance. He hasn't approached you at any time."

"But he still came after family!" she snapped.

"Only because Ian contacted him. Not because of you." Samson pressed a kiss to her temple. "We're safe, sweetheart. I won't let anything happen to you or Isaac."

August played the words through her head. He wasn't upset, but confident. She turned toward him, shrugging off his arm. "You knew!"

"Well . . ." Samson hedged.

August smacked him on the chest. "You let me run around like nothing was wrong and you knew David was still running loose."

Samson grasped her hands, firmly but gently. "Yes, I knew. I coordinated with a few friends, as well as Joshua Hastings, to make sure we were safe. He has a security firm and offered his assistance"

"And on that note, I will let the two of you work this out." Sgt. Falls stood up to leave.

"Oh no, you don't," she protested. "You may want to witness or protect him."

Sgt. Falls chuckled. "Ma'am, I make it a practice not to get involved in domestic situations. They're much too volatile for my sake."

Samson stood up. "I'll see you out, Falls," he said.

August crossed her arms as she flopped back on the cushions. *How dare the man withhold this information from me.* David hadn't been dangerous at first, not when he brought his dog Misty for training. But somewhere along the line, he'd developed an unhealthy fascination with August she didn't return. He ended up sending a bomb to her place, as well as the pet grooming salon next door, as a way to encourage favor.

The entire fiasco finally ended when he attacked her, and she'd shoved poop in his face to escape; it was the second scariest moment in her life.

A chime signaled the front door opened and closed. A whir and click announced the door was locked again and the alarm set. Shuffling footsteps preceded Samson's entrance.

"I'm upset with you," she announced.

Next to her, the cushion dipped beneath his weight. "I know," he stated quietly. "You were already so frazzled when we found out he escaped; it was easier to bring you a small measure of peace while I figured this out."

"Seriously, Samson. You can't keep things like this from me. We have a child."

"I know. I'd already put you through so much, I wanted to carry this burden, hoping the cops would catch him before he did anything else." He grazed his knuckles along her cheek. "You were always safe."

She brushed his hand away, but it was half-hearted.

"Just so you know I'm glaring at you."

He chuckled. "I can feel my face singeing." He tugged her into his arms. "I'm sorry for not telling you."

She pushed against him. "Don't use that sweet voice on me," she admonished.

"Why not?"

"Because it's working."

He slipped a hand beneath her shirt, encountering warm skin. "You've got abs."

She slipped her hand under his shirt. "So do you."

He ravished her mouth with a heart-stopping kiss. "Let me make it up to you."

"In the bedroom," she whispered against his lips. "Isaac could see us."

Laughing, he stood up, drawing her to her feet. "C'mon, lover; let me take you to paradise."

⌒

"And go!" Sam yelled over the pulsing music.

"How many squats?" August grumbled between gritted teeth.

Jason laughed. "It ain't that bad, sexy," he stated.

"You're too darn cheerful," she muttered.

"Don't mind her," Samson said from the other side of Jason. "She didn't get much sleep last night."

"And rest!"

Resting consisted of them sitting on an exercise bench, grasping a pair of dumbbells for shoulder presses.

"Less talking. More counting," Troy called.

"Does it matter how many we do?" August shot back. "It's what we can do in a minute."

"Oo, somebody's sassy today," Troy quipped.

"Somebody's mouthy today too," she retorted.

Jason barked a laugh, as did the others; it was good they had this workout today. After everything he'd experienced over the week, he needed the vigor of a workout. A slow smile creased his lips as he recalled that he'd gotten plenty of exercise with GG last night.

"You doin' way too much smilin' sandbag," Troy ribbed Jason.

Jason laughed but kept pumping weights. His shoulders were singing with the effort.

"And go!"

He laid back and anchored his feet, then brought his arms wide, as if going for a hug, before bringing the weights together in a chest press.

An hour later, Jason crowded August. She poked him in his very sore pecs. He grasped her finger and kissed it.

"Now you don't go giving me that tenderness either," she scolded. "I worry about you, and now the crazy asshole who was bothering me is out for you too."

"You must really be upset if you're swearing," Jason teased.

She tried to snatch her hand away, but he held on. "You bet your sweet hippy."

He cracked up and drew her close in a tight hug.

"Ew! You're all sweaty."

"So are you." He cupped her cheek and dropped a kiss on her upturned mouth. "You helped me be safe with the cameras and the alarm. If not for that, we wouldn't know who was behind the sabotage."

"I thought you and August were together," an unfamiliar female voice stated to Samson.

"We are," Samson answered. "Is Jason smooching her again?"

"Mind your business," August said in a sing-song voice.

Jason laughed. "Be nice," he admonished.

"I am," she retorted. "What's really gonna blow her mind is when she sees you with GG."

"Here, love," Samson brushed her arm with her coat and helped her into the garment.

"Thanks," she leaned over and kissed Samson.

"Crazy poly people," Troy muttered.

"That's us," Jason grinned. "Now let's go to lunch."

Chapter Eleven

David Foster Marsh deftly taped the timer in place. He didn't need anything sophisticated for this round of things to go boom; he only needed it to set fire. He placed his incendiary device aside and closed his eyes, thinking of his stupid sister and her sense of nobility. Had she only left things alone, she would still be alive, not scattered all over the Ann Arbor landscape.

David stood, staring at a picture of a trim woman with long sister locks and a wide easy smile, holding the leash of a yellow Labrador. He touched the photo with reverent fingertips. He loved August; this was the woman he wanted to spend the rest of his life with, the woman he called his angel. And she rejected him. Every bomb he planted was for her, to make her fall in love with him for his heroism in saving her.

It almost worked too, with the bomb he'd sent to her at the dog training center after months of getting to know her with his own dog, Misty. He'd warned her, which had garnered him her gratitude, but she was involved with the stupid cop, the cop his sister had loved. She'd given her life to save him.

And now he was going to kill the cop and everyone who August loved. If he couldn't have August River, then no one would.

While he was at it, he'd make sure the other blind man was out of the picture too. If he was going back to prison, he'd make sure he had a high body count.

"The permits are still good on the trailer," GG announced, walking into the kitchen where the scent of sage and brown sugar clung to the air.

"I told you it was," Jason called back.

"I had to make sure since we haven't used it in a few months."

"Well, my ever-efficient partner makes sure all permits, licenses, and insurance are current and up-to-date."

"That I do," she chuckled. She walked toward the stove where he stood, stirring a pot of something. "What are you making?"

"Busy work," he answered. "Thought I would experiment with a new recipe or two."

"Do you have time to do that and cook for the event tomorrow?"

He laughed, the booming laugh that always curled her toes and made her want to join in the joke. "I do." He frowned. "I want to use this for our brunch Sunday. Tell me what's missing." He removed a plastic spoon from the many in his chef's coat pocket, scooped out a bit of the hot liquid, and held it out to GG.

GG grasped his hand and brought the spoon to her lips. She blew across the bowl and took a tentative taste.

Butter, brown sugar, and vanilla exploded across her tongue. She rolled the mixture around in her mouth. Now she got notes of cardamon, cinnamon, and she flicked another sample into her mouth, *was that a hint of nutmeg? What was this missing?*

"Depending on what you're going for, you can add some fresh ginger to the mix. Other than that, I like it."

Jason nodded. "I'll make it both ways. Was thinking of using this as a sauce."

She removed the spoon from his hand and tossed it in a nearby trashcan. She ran her fingers over his bare wrist and up the sleeve of his jacket. Touching him in this way was pleasurable. She closed her eyes, savoring the texture and feel of the man.

"You're trying to start something."

She turned the burner off. "I can finish this." She slipped between him and the stove. "You know what excites me the most about being here with you?" She played her fingers over his jawline, traced his lips before going on her tiptoes to follow with her lips.

"What?"

"Being able to touch and tease you whenever the mood strikes." She kissed his mouth, not at all surprised at his receptiveness. He allowed her to lead the kiss, probing and teasing. She deepened the kiss, enjoying the smooth, masculine taste of him, and leaned into him as his arms circled her waist. He pressed into her, shifting slightly so her back was against the cool of the cabinet.

How long had she pined after this man, watching him interact with his other women and wishing she could be a part of his life, at least more than his sous chef. Now she was kissing him, touching him, sharing his bed and home as if they were made for one another.

"GG," he whispered against her lips.

"Hmm?" She worked the buttons on his chef's coat until she reached the long-sleeved shirt beneath. "I love your body."

He lifted her, settling her on the countertop. He stood in the vee of her thighs. "You drive me wild."

Chuckling, she stroked the nape of his neck, fascinated at the softness of his hair. "Did you know you've got lots of little curls and coils back here?"

"Is that a nice way of saying I've got a nappy head?"

She laughed. "If that was the case, I'd have said so."

A chime rang out, alerting them to an impending visitor. Jason stepped back, buttoning his jacket as GG hopped off the counter, straightening her own clothes.

"Am I interrupting?" Alistair clomped into the kitchen.

"Not at all," GG said as nonchalantly as possible.

"Then why are you blushing?"

She shot him a murderous look, and he only grinned. "It's hot in the kitchen."

"I'll say it is," Jason murmured, brushing past her and returning to the stove.

Alistair snorted. "You two are so cute. Making out in the kitchen." He donned an apron. "I could leave and come back in like thirty minutes, if that works."

Jason laughed. "Very kind of you to offer," he shot back as he flicked on the burner.

"Don't encourage him," GG snapped good-naturedly.

"What smells good? A new recipe?" Alistair thankfully dropped the subject.

GG smoothed a hand over her hair before walking to the clipboard she'd set down earlier. "We've got a couple of events this weekend."

"I saw the trailer outside," Alistair said. "Brings back memories of the good old days."

"Indeed," Jason commented. "I spent the morning getting it ready."

"And I spent the morning making sure we could actually use it." GG rolled her eyes. "We're good to go."

"Any word on when we'll get a new food truck?" Alistair held his hand out for the clipboard. GG placed a couple of sheets of paper into his hand. He looked these over before walking toward the pantry.

"Got the specs in," Jason said. "Should hear something in a week or so."

"Make sure it has a little more elbow room and a better counter," he called, his voice muffled.

"Already taken into account," Jason said. To GG, he said, "Ginger, huh?"

"Just a smidge," she agreed. GG watched as Jason walked across the kitchen to the walk-in. He disappeared a moment, then returned with the tan knobby root in his hand. A thought occurred, and a hot flash heated her body. *Would he be receptive to something so...lurid?* She licked her lips as once more desire pulsed between her legs. Hell, since professing her feelings for Jason, she'd been in a constant state of arousal. Only his thorough lovemaking assuaged her wantonness—at least for a time.

Chapter Twelve

Samson sat in the dark. The only reason he knew it was dark was his remaining eye was not stinging. Ever since the explosion, which claimed an eye and his eyesight, light, any type of light, bothered him. At first the sunglasses were to hide the fact he was missing an eye. He didn't want to go through life with an eyepatch, no matter how cool Nick Fury made it look. The prosthetic one he now wore still felt foreign in the empty socket, but it gave the illusion he still had two eyes.

He rested his hands, palms side up on his knees, and slowly inhaled for four, then exhaled for four. He repeated this several times Tension eased from his shoulders in slow degrees. *David was after Sol again.*

Inhale.

Exhale.

Tension gripped his shoulders and squeezed. *How am I going to protect Sol and Isaac when I can't ever see an attack coming?*

Inhale.

Exhale.

He'd gotten lucky the first time he took down David, but he didn't think he'd get lucky a second time. He rotated his head from side to side. Bones popped and cracked as he released more tension. Stx promised to keep Sol and Isaac safe and needed to keep that promise.

He allowed his chin to drop on his chest. Sol was right; he should've told her she was still in danger. But he'd hoped, really believed, David would be back behind bars by now. After all, Rodney and the others had been apprehended or killed. Those threats had been eliminated, but not David.

Stx wracked his brain, turning over each memory he had of the interaction between David and Sol. She'd been friendly, but not overly so. Pleasant and warm, but again not overly so. He couldn't remember anything Sol had done to encourage David. Then again, Sol was the type of woman men wanted either in bed or as a wife. She had that type of vibe about her; even Stx wanted to spend the rest of his life with her and would do anything to make that happen. And he would protect and defend her at all costs, sight or no sight.

Overhead boards creaked. Stx cocked his head to the side, listening to the soft footsteps. They descended the stairs, paused as one foot scuffed the tile, and then were muffled on the large rug. Brown sugar trickled up his nostrils, and all the tightness left his muscles to pool in his groin.

"Little boy is down for the count." She drifted her hand over the sofa until she brushed his leg, then straddled him. He rested his hands on her hips. "Which means we have some time to ourselves."

He brushed a kiss over her mouth. "Do we now?" he queried. He worked his fingers beneath the hem of her shirt. Her skin was warm and soft. He continued lifting the material until he uncovered one pert nipple and laved the tip, relishing the sigh filling the air.

"We should really do this in the room," August said breathlessly.

He switched to her other nipple, while he pulled down the waistband of her pajama bottoms. Her scent beckoned. He stroked her heat, satisfied to find her wet for him, always ready for him. He slipped two fingers inside her tightness, stroking and mimicking what his dick was going to do to her. She rode his hand as he sucked her nipples.

"Samson," she hissed. "Please."

He chuckled. "Then stay quiet," he admonished. "And you won't wake the kid." He shifted her enough to remove her bottoms, then positioned her over the head of his cock. He thrust up as he pulled her down on him. He pressed his mouth to hers, gulping down her moan of pleasure.

He closed his eyes, savoring the tight way she gripped him. No matter how many times they made love, she was always tight for him. His fingers dug into her butt as he thrust into her, pounding her heat until she clung to him. Her pussy held his cock in a stranglehold, massaging and gripping with every stroke. She stiffened in his arms; her cry muffled in the hollow of his shoulder. He pressed his face into her neck as he spasmed, filling her with his cum. They sat there, panting and holding one another, as tiny aftershocks rocked their bodies.

"Hold on to me," he coaxed.

She tightened her limbs around him as he stood. Carefully, he navigated to the bedroom. She closed the door before he continued to the bed. Together, they fell on the mattress, and his cock swelled inside her. He grasped her hands and held them above her head, as he pounded into her pliant heat. He loved how she gave herself to him. No matter if it was a few minutes in the shower, a stolen moment in the kitchen, or like they were on the living room sofa, she gave. He would keep her safe. He would keep them all safe.

Burning leaves, spiced cider, and the fragrant scent of yeast rose on the crisp October air. Jason sniffed appreciatively as he arranged handfuls of soaked wood chips on the grill. Today he was using a combination of pecan and cherry. Indistinct voices as well as laughter laced with the throaty roar of motorcycles and generators wound around him. From the sounds of things, the Fall Spookactular was a success.

"You doing all right?" GG sidled next to him.

"Of course, love. Just taking in the atmosphere." He dug in his apron pocket for the long-handled lighter and set it to the bit of kindling in the chimney. A few minutes later, he removed the cylindrical device and allowed the fire to spread in the pit.

"You haven't lost your touch." A bit of awe clung to her voice.

"Thanks." With practiced ease, he settled the grates back in place. The heat welcomed against the autumn chill. "How are we doing on orders?"

"Alistair is wowing the crowd with his comedic prowess."

Jason barked a laugh. "Then I better hurry and get this grill going again before we lose our customers."

"I heard that," Alistair said walking up. "I'll have you know I've fifteen orders ready when you've got the burgers and dogs going."

Jason opened a door at knee level and pulled out a sleeve of burgers. He quickly laid down the patties, then erected a fire and heatproof barrier. He laid out several brats, then dogs.

"You're so good at that it's scary," Alistair commented.

"Practice." Jason shrugged. He opened his mouth to say more but felt GG stiffen beside him. "What is it?"

"Uh, hi," a tentative male voice began.

"What do you want?" GG demanded in an icy tone.

"Uh, I had no idea what Ian was up to," the tentative male voice began.

The smooth tenor, the polite resonance, Jason knew who was speaking. "Dylan."

"Uh yeah," Dylan answered. "I won't stay long but wanted to say how sorry I am for what happened. I didn't realize Ian was so obsessed with being number one."

Defeat and utter embarrassment clung to the other man's voice. There were a few other emotions Jason couldn't quite decipher, but the remorseful tone was enough. "I didn't even know we had a feud going with you guys," Jason stated lightly.

Dylan's laugh was brief and brittle. "He thought you had a leg up because of your vision. I told him that was silly. Your food is really, really good. We're just in different markets."

When GG stepped forward, Jason laid a hand on her shoulder. He gave it a reassuring squeeze. "This has to be hard on you as well, knowing your partner was arrested."

"Yes." A sniffle. "He was arrested in the middle of a rush. I've had to scramble the last few days to get extra help but," he trailed off. "It's not the same as having to replace your entire food truck. For what it's worth, I'm sorry."

"Thanks, Dylan. But you're not the one at fault," Jason pointed out gently. "Your apology is appreciated all the same."

"Thanks."

Again, GG stiffened beneath his hand, and Jason squeezed her again. He went back to the grill, flipping the items over.

"Why did you absolve him?" GG demanded all fiery temper. "You could've been killed with Ian's stunts!"

"True, but clearly Dylan wasn't the mastermind behind the plot. He's collateral damage." Carefully, he shifted the burgers and dogs around. "Didn't you hear the anguish in his voice?"

"Well, yeah," she answered warily.

"We only have to replace a truck; Dylan won't be able to replace his partner or reputation so easy."

"I hate it when you make sense," she grumbled. "He looked pretty miserable too."

"No doubt."

"Hey, GG," Alistair called. "I'm gonna need you up front."

"Duty calls." She patted his butt.

He laughed. "We'll talk about that pat later," he promised huskily.

"I'm counting on it."

David bit into the loaded brat with gusto. He barely stifled the moan of pleasure as he chewed, as flavors he hadn't thought possible burst over his tongue. It was a sweetness he couldn't identify, coupled with a salty taste that complimented the smoky cheese, relish, and other condiments he'd heaped on the grilled sausage. A combination of juices and ketchup dribbled from the corner of his mouth. He licked it up, and what he couldn't get with his tongue he got with a wad of napkins.

Milling around, he blended into the crowd of people, when he first arrived at the event. Some stopped and considered the various food offerings, while others sampled or bargained over the arts and crafts available. David hedged closer to The Dog Hut, mildly surprised to find the food truck still up and running. If he'd known about the second vehicle, maybe he'd have blown that up too. Then again, if he had, he wouldn't be enjoying the truly delicious brat. He shoved a handful of still hot fries in his mouth. The food was so fresh, he had no idea it could taste so good.

David observed the tall, black man with the close-cropped hair. A fine sheen of sweat glistened on his forehead, as he flipped burgers or turned the slightly smiling dogs and brats. David tilted his head to the side, trying to figure out if the man was truly without sight or if he had some vision. Not that it mattered either way, but he was curious.

David knew August had a little bit of vision, mostly colors and shapes. However, she was completely reliant on visual aids and braille. He loved that about her. She was so smart and motivated to live.

But not with him.

David tossed his trash in a nearby barrel. August didn't find him to her liking, but she was attracted to this tall, blind man? The man could no longer drive! *What was it*

August saw in these men? Both the men she dated were blind. David snorted. He'd tried killing them both also.

He sidestepped a cop in a bulky sweater and gel-spiked hair. Carefully, he shifted the brim of his hat to shield more of his face.

The cop bypassed the long line of people in front of The Dog Hut and palmed his badge. The pretty woman waved him around back. David stepped to the back of the line, waiting his turn. While in line, he meandered to the menu board in hopes of catching any of the conversation.

Between the background noise, music, and traffic two blocks away, he couldn't make out much. Before he knew it, it was his turn at the window again, so this time he ordered a double bacon burger and more of the hand-cut fries. Now he could pace himself and maybe lurk closer to the grill where the tall man and cop were talking.

"...gave us the name..." the cop said.

A burst of laughter drowned out Jason's response.

Be —," then loud laughter occurred. "Not apprehended yet."

"I don't even know this guy," Jason said.

David moved a little closer, being careful to keep a few people between him and the two men.

"You're familiar with August River?" the cop was saying.

David bit his lip, his heart racing at the mention of August's name. *Had Ian sold me out already? That would be the only reason for the cop to make the connection.*

"Of course. We date."

"He's the one who sent the bomb to her workplace. Ian admitted contracting him to help destroy your business."

David clenched his fists. He should've known he couldn't count on Ian to keep his mouth shut. It didn't matter anyway. If, and when, David went back to prison, he was looking at life behind bars. There would be no chance of parole; maybe a pardon if the orange man ever got re-elected, but he seriously doubted that would happen.

"Number 182," GG called. "Double bacon burger and fries."

David turned; that was his cue to leave. Smiling, he grabbed the bag from the pretty woman. Too bad she had to die too.

Chapter Thirteen

Sunday brunch turned into dinner. Jason grinned as he sat at the head of the square table. There were beautiful women on his left and right, with Stx sitting opposite. He rather liked the former police officer. The man had a great sense of humor, which was a perfect foil to August's snarky demeanor.

"This is so good!" August gushed. "The flavors make my mouth dance."

Jason laughed. "Thanks." Warmth enveloped him at her praise. He truly enjoyed feeding people, especially the ones he loved.

"Yeah, man, I don't think I've ever had anything like this before," Stx put in. "How did you get the beef so tender?"

"Low and slow," Jason answered. "And I let it marinate for a couple of days." He placed a hand over August's. "Was the beef too much for you?"

She squeezed his fingers. "You mean the quarter-size portion you placed on my plate?" she asked sarcastically. "Not at all."

GG laughed. "I'm not a big beef-eater either," she stated. "I thought the crab-stuffed salmon was more fitting."

"Was that your idea?" August asked.

"I had input on the menu," GG answered. "But I did do dessert."

"Chocolate?" August asked hopefully.

"Absolutely."

The doorbell rang.

"Are you expecting anyone?" Jason asked.

"I am expecting a package," GG said, scraping back her chair. "I'll get the door while you get dessert."

"I can help clear dishes." August pushed back her chair, reaching for the empty plates. While August cleared dishes from the table, Jason moved into the kitchen.

"Can I do anything?" Samson called.

"Just sit there and look pretty," August called back.

Jason snickered. "What did you order?"

"Since we're getting a new truck, I thought it would be nice to update our logo a bit," GG answered, walking back into the room.

August rinsed off the dishes before placing them in the dishwasher. "Oh cool! What do they look like?"

"Let's have dessert first before I open the box," GG said. "I don't want anything to interrupt the big reveal."

Shuffling feet drew attention toward the door. "Do you smell something burning?" Samson asked.

"One of the neighbors is burning leaves," GG said dismissively. "I caught the smoke when I opened the door."

"Anybody want coffee?" August asked.

"I thought you'd never ask," Samson said dramatically.

They laughed.

"Haven't you had enough caffeine for the day?" she teased. "I remember you inhaling half a pot this morning before breakfast."

"That was breakfast," Samson told her.

Jason laughed at the easy banter. Things hadn't always been this easy between them, at least not at first. It was several months before Jason sensed Stx was comfortable with his presence and role in August's life. Jason had no desire to monopolize August's time or heart; he wanted to share a part in her life.

Dishes rattled while fresh ground Italian roast filled the air. A hand clapped Jason on the back.

"I knew there was a reason I liked you," Samson stated.

"Other than my food?"

He laughed. "You have the best coffee."

Jason laughed, before handing him a bowl. "Try it with dessert and tell me what you think."

Samson made his way back to the dining room table. A moment later, August set a mug of hot coffee near his right hand. "Thanks, babe." He squeezed her fingers before she could leave.

She brushed her free hand over his cheek. "Anytime, love." She settled next to him.

"They're so cute," GG murmured, as she leaned into Jason.

He shifted so he could drape one arm over her shoulders. "Yeah. They love each other a great deal."

"How do you not get jealous?" she wondered.

He kissed the top of her head. "I have a great love right here in my arms. Why do I need to be jealous?" he countered. He cinched her tighter. "Or are you feeling a little jealous?"

GG opened her mouth to deny it, then stopped. "Maybe a little," she admitted in a small voice. "But I realize we're still so new, and I'm uncertain."

He caressed her cheek. "Thank you for telling me." He brushed his lips over hers. "Whenever you feel like that, please let me know. I wanted you to meet August and Stx so you would know she could never replace who you are to me. And you can see she's not interested in replacing who you are to me."

"But she can relate to you in a way I can't," GG blurted.

He furrowed his brow. "How so?"

"She knows what it's like for you to lose your sight. She can relate to that. She can say and do things I can't."

"Oh, Greta." He kissed her softly. "You've known me for a very long time. You stuck by me when others left. You've known me before and after the accident. August only knows me as a blind man. Some days, I have no idea why you want to be with me."

"You're the same man I fell in love with all those years ago. Nothing has changed that, only made my love stronger."

"Exactly. Be who you are," he told her. "That's all I ask. Be the woman who loves me for who I am. All I want to do is love you for who you are."

She raised on her tiptoes to kiss him. He reached down and grabbed a handful of her ass. "Be nice," she chuckled.

"I am." He grinned against her lips. "Let's finish our coffee and dessert."

They lingered at the table long after dessert was eaten. Laughter and a genial camaraderie settled through the group. GG cast a grateful glance around the people present and felt settled. She could get used to this.

"I thought you were bringing Isaac with you," she said suddenly.

August laughed. "That was the plan until his brother showed up and said he had tickets to the new Paw Patrol show."

"Sadly, Uncle Jason is no match for Chase and Rubble," Stx sighed for dramatic effect.

They laughed.

"So, what did you get for the food truck?" Jason prompted.

"Oh. Right." GG pushed back her chair. A moment later, she returned with the box and thumped it on the table.

Jason sniffed. "You smell that?"

The others sniffed the air. "That doesn't smell like leaves burning," August said. Beside her, Samson squeezed her hand. She winced. "What's the matter?"

"There's smoke!" GG cried. "Did we leave the stove on?"

Jason coughed. "No. I didn't use the stove for the desserts."

"Samson?" August asked quietly. "What's the matter?"

Stx sat still. The scent of almonds was so strong, only the odor of burning metal and ash was stronger. He blinked several times. Sol's voice seemed to come to him from a great tunnel. Something cool and soft touched his face. He turned his cheek into a gentle hand. No, he wasn't back in the training room where he lost his sight and his partner. He was sitting in a friend's dining room, with August.

With a bomb.

Stx licked dry lips. "We need to get out of here," he stated, surprised at how calm he sounded.

"What is it?" Jason demanded. He stood so fast, his chair clattered to the floor.

Glass shattered a moment before something whooshed and hissed. Another crash followed the first.

"What was that?" August demanded, tugging Samson to his feet.

"Somebody just threw Molotov cocktails through the front window," GG shouted her voice, a little strained.

"Close the door and we'll go out the back," Jason said calmly.

Coughing, GG ran to close the door between the living and dining rooms; that would give them time.

Smoke was quickly filling the air as the four made their way to the back door. Jason touched the knob, checking that the door wasn't hot. He opened it.

GG, who was standing just behind Jason, caught movement from the corner of her eye. Without thinking, she shoved Jason aside.

Pain exploded in her right side.

"Don't go out there!" she gasped. "Somebody's out there!"

"That was a gunshot!" Samson yelled. He crawled forward, slamming the door closed as another bullet vibrated the door's thick wood. He reached up, fumbling for the locks and threw the bolt.

"Who's shooting?" Jason demanded.

"We need to get out of here!" Samson said.

"The sliders," Jason suggested.

"Stay low, and keep your nose and mouth covered as much as possible," Samson ordered. "Sol?"

Coughing, she tapped his calf. "Where are the sliders?"

"Off the dining room," Jason said between coughs. "The table sits directly in front of the doors."

"All right. Let's move. Everybody stay low."

"GG?" Jason called. "Baby, where are you?"

No answer.

Fabric rustled as Samson and August crawled ahead. The low smoke rapidly filled the house and heat washed over them. As they entered the dining area, the heat intensified. Samson moved a hand in front of him, bumping one of the table legs. He paused long enough to get his location and sat against the wall. He flung out his left hand and caught wall board. Just a few more feet.

Something soft touched his face. He'd made it to the sliders and pressed a hand to the glass, surprised to find it warm. Heart hammering, he realized with horror they were trapped.

"What is it?" August asked.

"We're trapped!" he whispered.

An anguished howl rose behind them.

"She's dead!" Jason roared. "Oh gosh, she's dead."

Jason couldn't think, but just cradled GG's still body in his lap. She wasn't moving, and his hands were shaking too bad to even realize she was breathing.

Of all the things he'd been through in his life, he didn't think he could make it without GG. No, he knew his life wouldn't be the same without her in it. They'd been a team for so long: first in the restaurant, now in the food truck business, and their new emotional and physical connection. He would not recover from the loss of this love.

Someone was talking to him. He shook his head, continuing to rock GG in his arms.

"Dammit, Jason!"

The expletive cut through the fog of grief. Sol seldom swore. "Stop swearing at me!"

"I'll keep swearing at you until you start listening to me," she snapped. "She's not dead; she's unconscious."

Not dead? He allowed those two words to wash over and through him. Not. Dead. GG was still alive. Now he roamed his hands over her body. The steady rise and fall beneath his palms told him the truth. He moved upward, encountering a hot and sticky liquid. The metallic tang of blood filled his nostrils. "She's hurt."

Coarse material draped over his hand. Quickly, he folded the towel and pressed it against the wound. Still, GG did not move.

"Samson says we can't get out through the sliders," she murmured.

"And if we try to go out the doors, we risk getting shot."

"August, I need you in here," Samson called.

"Keep her warm. The wound doesn't seem to be bleeding a lot but keep pressure on it just in case," August said before she crawled toward Samson's voice.

"Uh, don't you think you should have the bomb squad handle this?" Joshua Hastings was saying. Amusement tinged the voice sliding from the phone speaker.

"Hell yeah," Samson agreed. "In the meantime, we're trapped in a burning house with a shooter on the outside."

"Damn," Joshua whistled.

"Right. GG has been hit. Now I need your eyes so I can disarm this bomb. Hopefully keep us all alive until the fire department can rescue us."

"What can I do?" August asked, stifling a cough.

"Hold the phone so I can work," Samson ordered. "Move it the way Joshua tells you."

"But."

"We are not leaving Isaac an orphan; he will not lose us," he said, his tone emphatic. "We can do this because I'm not gonna let David kill my family."

"Move to the left," Joshua instructed, his voice calm. "I see three wires. One green, red, and yellow."

"Is there a timer?"

"Pull back a little."

August did, keeping her movements steady despite the tremor in her hands.

"You've got plenty of time," Joshua said. "Your left hand is on the green wire. It's attached to the timer. Pan over the box for me, August."

She did as instructed.

"If you strip and clip, starting with the green wire, you should be good."

"Should?" August croaked and immediately started hacking.

Despite the situation, Samson smiled. "Josh is being funny, love," he explained. "If David wanted this puppy to blow, he'd have made it more challenging."

"Y'all have a weird sense of humor," she grumbled.

Smiling, Samson carefully stripped the wire, exposing the filament beneath the plastic coating. He did the same on the other two.

Sirens whined in the distance. A small explosion brought the roar of flames closer, as heat shoved its way in until it filled the room. Smoke swirled, choking them.

Samson coughed. August sat next to him, but she still coughed. They need oxygen and to get out of this blasted house.

"We need to get lower, under the smoke," Samson told her.

"Okay," she croaked.

Samson carefully moved the box to the floor. Here the air was marginally better, but not much.

"It's getting hot in here!" Jason called.

The wail of sirens grew louder over the roar of the flames.

Ominous creaking, followed by a crash that shook the house, drew a small shriek from August.

"Keep it steady," he encouraged, clipping the first wire.

"Now the next," Joshua said.

Samson clipped the next.

"That's it!" Joshua shouted. "Now get the hell outta there."

Samson grabbed Sol's hand. "C'mon. Back to the kitchen." Coughing, they crawled. Behind them, something else popped and fell. Great tongues of heat poured over them. There was no air; it was simply too hot to breathe. Samson shoved Sol closer to the kitchen. If he could just get her out the door, then he could still keep his promise to her.

Hissing rivaled the roar of flames. He felt droplets of sweat or was it water misted over his face? He couldn't tell. What he did know was August wasn't breathing.

Epilogue

"Thank you all for coming to the re-grand opening of The Dog Hut!" GG announced to a crowd of hungry patrons. There were well over a hundred people ready and willing. She adjusted the sling her right arm rested in; it would be another week before she could lose the irritating device. She looked over her shoulder at the shiny new food truck. Every surface on the vehicle gleamed; even the hubcaps shone. Students from U of M's culinary program roamed through the crowd with samples of the food.

"The crowd is amazing!" GG said, excitement in her voice. "I had no idea we had this many fans."

Jason curved an arm at her waist. "We have good food and service," he answered.

She leaned into him. "I can't believe we're alive to enjoy all of this."

Jason kissed the top of her head; he couldn't either. The shooting, fire, and near bombing a few weeks before seemed like someone else's life. Had GG not pushed him out of the way, he'd have been the one injured. She'd literally taken a bullet for him.

"What made you push me out of the way?"

"The first time you were injured, I was too far away to do anything," she stated, her words measured. "This time, I could do something. I couldn't bear to see you hurt again."

"If I'd have lost you, there wouldn't be anyone to pick up the pieces."

With her good hand, she smoothed down his shirt. "A good poly man like you? You'd be deep and inconsolable for about ten minutes, then move on."

He threw back his head and laughed at her teasing. "It would take me more than ten minutes to get over you. More like ten lifetimes."

A cover of Kool and the Gang's "Celebration" filled the silence. "GG....," Jason stated.

"There you are!" A pint-size person flung his arms around Jason's waist, nearly knocking him over.

"Isaac!" Jason patted the boy on the back while he regained his balance.

"Ma said you and Aunt GG were having a grand opening on your new truck! She said you got new food too. Can I have a hot dog? With ketchup and that melty cheese?"

"Sure."

"Isaac," August admonished. "You just had a snack."

"He's okay, Sol," Jason said. "I'll get his hot dog." That was another thing he could be grateful for: August and Stx were safe, although August stayed a few extra days in the hospital due to smoke inhalation. It had been touch and go for a bit. He gripped her hand. "How are you?"

She chuckled. "Just fine. Still have to blow into that stupid breathing thing, but it's fine."

"Not fine," Samson put in. "She gets winded going up and down the steps."

August stepped closer to Jason. "Have you had a chance to ask her yet?"

"Not yet."

"Ask me what?" GG wanted to know.

Jason patted his pockets to make sure he had what he needed before bending to one knee before GG. He stifled a smile at GG's audible gasp.

"You make me happy. No other woman has ever brought the question of marriage into my mind or heart, except you. I love many and will continue to do so, but I only desire one wife to share the rest of my life. Would you do me the honor of being my wife?"

Around them, the crowd and music seemed to fade into silence. For a long moment, Jason held his breath and waited.

With trembling hands, GG rested her palm on Jason's cheek. She bent down and caressed his lips with hers. "I would love to be your wife."

A cheer rose up from the surrounding crowd. Jason surged to his feet, lifting GG and twirling her. He couldn't imagine a more perfect woman to love for the rest of his life.

Book Club Questions

1. Jason and August (from *Blind Fury*) enjoy a polyamorous lifestyle. What do you think of this lifestyle?

2. GG has an opportunity to move into Jason's position as head chef but chooses to follow Jason to be his partner in a food truck. Would you change careers to follow someone you love?

3. August, Stx, and Isaac, along with Jason and GG, all live with chosen families instead of biological relatives. What does this story say about family? How do you define family?

4. Ian chooses to not vandalize the inside of the food truck as he intended, but he still lets David do his part in the sabotage. What do you think of his change of heart?

Author Bio

Lynn Chantale, a romance novelist, short story writer, and part-time background singer, has published many stories across several genres. Her works include *Sex, Lies, and Joysticks*, *True Detective Series*, and *Broken Lens*, to name a few.

When she's not actively planning world domination, she's dominating her household, family, and her cat: Shakespeare. You can visit her at any of her cyber haunts:

Website:
https://www.thehouseoflynn.com

Twitter:
https://twitter.com/lynnchantale

Facebook:
https://www.facebook.com/LynnChantaleAuthor

Facebook Group Tale's Tells:
https://www.facebook.com/groups/talestells

Instagram:
https://www.instagram.com/lynn_chantale/

Youtube:
https://www.youtube.com/channel/
UCHbAParOHDB7cwfSwUtU3cA

More books from 4 Horsemen Publications

Romance

ANN SHEPPHIRD
The War Council

EMILY BUNNEY
All or Nothing
All the Way
All Night Long: Novella
All She Needs
Having it All
All at Once
All Together
All for Her

KT BOND
Back to Life
Back to Love
Back at Last

LYNN CHANTALE
The Baker's Touch
Blind Secrets
Broken Lens
Blind Fury
Time Bomb

VIP's Revenge
Chef's Taste

MANDY FATE
Love Me, Goaltender
Captain of My Heart

MIMI FRANCIS
Private Lives
Private Protection
Private Party
Run Away Home
The Professor
Our Two-Week, One
Night Stand

SHAE COON
Bound in Love
Controlling Assets
For His Own Protection
Her Broken Pieces
The Roma's Claim
The Roma's Promise

* 9 7 9 8 8 2 3 2 0 0 7 0 7 *